I0552150

Scissors in Her Hand

A novel by

Sisko Linduska

ISBN 978-1-7382535-0-0

Library and Archives of Canada Act 2004

Cover design by LE Pietarinen

Inspired by

Sav and Cher

Chapter 1
Cutting Along the Lines

She was never told she was beautiful when she was growing up. In another era, she would have been a common peasant girl. Her parents married in the old country in a simple outdoor ceremony attended only by the bride's brother, and a sister of the groom. With the promise of job opportunities and a landscape reminiscent of their homeland, Sullo and Myra abandoned everything they knew to begin a new life in a new world.

He had been a lumberjack in the old country when horse and sled were still used to haul logs to the sawmill. Myra's father married his mistress after divorcing and exiling her mother. She got away from her cruel and manipulative stepmother by taking work as a seamstress and gaining her independence while still a teenager.

Of course, their children didn't learn anything about the life their parents left behind until much later. There were no grandparents to pass on that history and Myra was tight-lipped, many things being kept secret. As young newlyweds, all they had was each other and what they could carry when they landed on the Atlantic shores of Canada. Neither could even say yes or no in English.

Sullo quickly found work in the northern logging camps of Manitoba while Myra stayed home having babies. Later, they moved from town to town as Sullo gained experience and expertise in carpentry. Once he joined the union and became a foreman they were able to settle in one place. By then they had two boys, Patrick and Billy. Billy was ten years old when Greta was born and Jesse came along three years after that. Greta was the blue-eyed blonde child that her parents always wanted. These were the Aryan qualities they found most desirable.

When Greta was a youngster her father worked days and her mother worked nights. There was no one home when she got home from school. Jesse went straight to the basement to watch tv when she arrived. Dad, who they called Isa had taught Greta how to mix a screwdriver, a shot of vodka over ice, in a short glass with orange juice. He drank as he waited for Greta to plate his dinner. There was warm meat in the oven her mother had prepared before going to work. Greta boiled the potatoes and served them with meat and broth from the oven. Sometimes he would dump a pocketful of coins on the table.

"If you can guess how much there is, you can keep it," he said.

His conversational English and pronunciation were quite good because of his exposure to the language through work but his thick Finnish accent would never go away.

Greta counted the coins while her dad ate, sparing him the trouble of doing it himself. Not surprisingly, she never did guess the correct amount of her dad's lunchtime poker winnings. Most days though, he ate alone, bathed in the sauna, and either did chores or watched tv until he went to bed.

Every weekend the whole family went to camp. That's what people called their cottage up North. In the summer, Greta's parents stayed in town to work while an older sibling or Aunt Esther was left to watch over the girls.

Billy was left in charge of Greta and her friend Sasha one week while Jesse stayed in town at a friend's. Greta and Sasha were best friends from kindergarten to grade eight, and for Greta, Sasha was the first person she kissed on the mouth. It only happened once as an experiment and it never changed their friendship.

Time was irrelevant in those days at camp when there wasn't a care in the world. Greta and Sasha canoed, swam for hours, explored nature and were never hungry. The most excitement for them that week was when a fierce storm began to loom over the lake. They watched from the camp window as the sky darkened.

Billy had left the girls alone to visit a friend down the road at another camp. It was early afternoon and they watched the water getting choppier, and choppier. The skies were dark grey and the powerful winds caused white caps to dance on the lake. The fishing boat that was tied to the dock began banging against it with each punishing wave. The girls worried as the gap between the boat and the dock widened. In a panic, they jumped into action to save the boat. Neither was strong enough to secure the ropes. So they held on with their little bodies to keep it from getting swept away by the thrashing waves.

Greta knew which camp Billy was at, so she left Sasha holding the boat while she ran as fast as she could to tell Billy what was happening. She never saw Billy's lithe body run so fast as it did that day in what was now a torrential downpour. Kicking mud from his heels, Billy raced in time to relieve Sasha and secure the boat. A disaster had been averted before she ran out of rope.

Most days weren't quite so exciting. They were carefree, spent lazing about applying sunscreen, wearing wide brimmed straw hats, drinking Kool-Aid through bendy straws, reading books, exploring, and catching bugs. If it rained, they still swam, as long as there wasn't lightning. Any other weather that kept them from being outside was simply met with cards, board games, more reading, and listening to the radio if a station would come through. There was no phone, no tv, and the fireplace was lit whenever there was a chill in the air. These were the best days of Greta's life and were indelibly etched on the fabric of her mind.

When Aunt Esther was at camp she always found things for Greta and Jesse to do. She brought her sewing machine and materials, scattering various tasks throughout the camp. Pins, patterns, fabrics, measuring tape, chalk, and scissors were a few of the supplies and notions Aunt Esther used for her creations.

Jesse was coddled because she was the baby of the family but Aunt Esther gave Greta serious jobs, like pinning patterns to fabric. She showed her how to cut the fabric along the guidelines of the patterns very carefully. Those were special scissors and were never to be used to cut anything other than fabric. Greta aspired to be as grown up, stylish, and sophisticated as her auntie. Esther wasn't just a role model Greta emulated. She was Sullo's baby sister who emigrated several years after Greta's parents did, and she believed in rules.

Since Greta and her sister were still quite young, they weren't expected to use the outhouse after dark. It was a scary path to take at night even with a flashlight in hand. So the girls were still allowed to use a potty. However, at dawn, Aunt Esther made sure Greta carried the potty to the outhouse to empty its contents. One such morning, Greta peed and pooped in the potty upon waking up. On her way to dump it in the outhouse, she tripped, sending the poopy pissy potty flying up in the air. Her head was covered with warm urine and feces. She cried over the messy matter and her auntie made her wash herself, her clothes, and the shit stained potty in the lake.

Things were much different when Greta's parents were at camp on the weekends. Mom did chores, cooked, cleaned, and caught up on laundry which was hung on the line to dry. Dad chopped wood and taught Greta and Jesse how to fish. Jesse never developed a fondness for fishing or outdoorsy things the way Greta did.

There were times when their dad took Billy and Patrick fishing before dawn. They snuck out of the camp so they wouldn't wake mom and the girls, but Greta heard the outboard motor start and ran to the window. In the moonlight, she watched the boat sputter away with a single front headlight reflecting off the water. She wished they had taken her with them. When the boys got older, Sullo took them on week-long hunting trips into the deep forest. He never knew how close he was to not coming home as the boys plotted ways to kill him in the wilderness because of the physical abuse he did to them. As with many plans, they were never put into action.

Greta thought her dad was invincible. He built their camp from the ground up with the help of his sons who had no choice in the matter. To her, he was superhuman. He embodied Nordic ingenuity, could fix anything, and built innumerable things just from an idea. He was a hunter, fisherman and carpenter. He masterfully refinished furniture, pianos, and other musical instruments, built a fish smoker out a steel drum, and could get any motor running that wouldn't start.

He came home with everything from partridge to moose for the dinner table and raised their tarpaper bungalow to build a complete finished basement under it. When the basement was done, the original bungalow was moved back on top of the new solid foundation and the exterior was finished with brand new vinyl siding. They lived in the house while the basement was being built which made it seem like an adventure to Greta. They didn't have to borrow their neighbour's sauna anymore because they had a beautiful new indoor electric sauna in the new basement.

When she was little, nature was Greta's best friend. She did anything to not have to be in the house with her sister and mother. So she hung out in the garage with her dad, learning the names of the tools he asked her to pass him as she watch his work with amazement. How did he know so much about making things?

They went driving on the bush roads together when it was partridge season. When they brought the dead birds home, he showed her how to stand on their wings and pull up on their feet to get all the feathers off the meat. It was the leanest, cleanest meat she ever tasted and was especially good with lingonberry preserves.

One day, she accompanied her dad to their newest camp lot. So far, it was nothing more than a driveway on the wooded waterfront property. He used his chainsaw to cut down trees they dragged out of the bush to load onto the flatbed trailer. The logs were later taken to a sawmill and turned into lumber for their new dock. She was young and small but very strong and helped as much as any boy her age could, or more.

While loading one of the logs onto the trailer, it rolled onto her finger and her nail bed started to bleed. Greta said no more than an ouch and kept on going. Later in the truck, her dad asked about her finger and she said it was fine. He knew it was worse than she admitted because she sucked on it and hid it from him.

"The nail will probably fall off," he said calmly.

A few days later, it turned black and blue and eventually the nail fell off as he had said.

Greta, Jess, their parents and Aunt Esther all went blueberry picking one hot summer day. They walked through the thick brush and followed close behind one another as Sullo led the way. Greta had an underlying fear of getting lost.

As a woodsman, Sullo taught them to mind the branches being released by the person ahead. They walked with their hands up so they could catch flying branches. Getting struck stung like hell and each person was responsible for themselves not getting whipped in the face. They'd reach an opening in the forest where the big blue sky revealed a very large blueberry patch. The picking began.

Greta thought, what if a bear shows up? There was a nervous pinch in her gut because they were taking the bear's food. She stayed close to her dad, knowing he would save them from any old bear that might come along. And even though they were in the middle of the forest, he knew the way out. In fact, after their baskets and buckets were full, Sullo marched them out of the forest right back to where the truck was parked on the side of the dirt road. Greta figured he must have some sort of internal compass that gave him the ability to navigate the forest without getting lost. There were times, she learned, that her dad was not so perfect.

She was never quite sure what Jesse had done that day. They were at camp and their dad had been chopping firewood. Greta was helping stack the wood in a covered shelter. He piled the firewood on Greta's arms, up to her nose. As long as she could see over the bundle, she could handle the load. Her dad took a break as Greta continued stacking wood on her own. Then she heard something. Her dad was mad at Jesse. He made her fetch a branch off a bush.

"Go get a switch!" he demanded.

Jesse was already scared and whimpering, but she did as she was told and broke a branch off a bush she knew her dad would use on her. Greta could hear him whipping her as she squealed like a stuck piglet. Greta dared not say anything or do anything for fear he would turn his anger on her. Greta never knew why her dad switched her sister that day. What she heard only served to instill a heightened fear of crossing him.

One summer, Patrick earned his driver's license and bought a motorcycle with his own money. He was so proud of that bike and rode it to camp one weekend. Without permission, and after a few beers, Sullo took the bike for a ride down the dirt road. Meanwhile, Greta and Jesse were playing in the back of the homemade camper when they heard a commotion. Their dad was calling to his wife.

"Myra! Myra!" he wailed.

He limped to the camp holding one arm against his body. They heard Patrick go into a rage. Dad had crashed Patrick's brand new motorcycle!

Greta and Jesse huddled silently watching from the safety of the camper window. Patrick had every right to be mad and an irreparable rift was forged between father and son.

When things got tense Greta learned to lay low. If she stayed quiet and out of sight then she could avoid getting in trouble or becoming the subject of her father's wrath. She knew that if her brothers talked back to him, he wasn't averse to smacking them around and could lift one off the ground with one hand. He pinned Patrick to the wall once and threatened him with his fist. Then he flung him to the floor like a rag doll. Greta knew her dad's temper and yielded to the tone of his voice before he ever made an aggressive gesture towards her.

Greta's parents were arguing one time when she was quite little and her dad violently shoved Myra onto the bed. Holding her down with his left hand, he raised his right hand in a fist.

"Stop!!" little Greta shrieked at the top of her lungs.

He stopped, released his grip, and lowered his fist. How many times had he followed through when Greta wasn't there?

The events of her childhood would have far reaching impacts on the depths of her psyche, not to be realized until much later in a life.

Chapter 2
Mechanical Drudgery

Her mother was loving and tender at times, like when she gently placed Greta's head on her lap and scratched her scalp with a knitting needle. It made it that much harder to swallow her insidiously subtle and cruel sarcasm when it crept out. Greta would proudly come home from school with an A on a paper, test, or project.

"Where's the plus?" her mother asked.

If she got 95%, her mother would ask, "What happened to the other 5%?"

She utterly deflated. Getting good grades came easy for Greta, but her mother wanted an unattainable perfection. After a while, she realized it was an exercise in futility to strive for the impossible goal set by her mother. No matter what she did, it was never good enough. Eventually she gave up on trying to win her mother's approval and settled on passing grades that required no effort. She developed unhealthy insecurities about not being perfect which in reality were disproportionate to her abilities. She quit trying to excel at anything academic and began to focus purely on the social image she projected. Instead of trying to impress her mother she began to seek approval from other sources. After all, everyone needs to feel appreciated by someone.

The dilapidated piano Sullo gutted in their living room was transformed into a gleaming new instrument of burden. What was once a piece of junk now had new keys, and strings that had been finely tuned by a professional. The sisters promptly began weekly lessons, being required to practice at least an hour a day. Sixty minutes to a kid felt like an eternity. Their mother enlisted them in festivals, recitals, music camps, and exams until they both became proficient pianists. For Greta, being able to play the music technically was not analogous to finding pleasure in performing. Instead, it was her duty to make it to the next level.

Their mother constantly compared the girls to two boys who lived across the street. They were skilled and dedicated to the classical guitar. Their mom made sure to remind them at every chance of how talented those boys were. Her need to make the girls competitive produced resentment rather than music appreciation. She couldn't accept that talent and desire were innate and that prodigious musicians were born, not made.

Doug and Erik were rigid high achieving students and Greta began to harbor serious animosity towards them. She picked on them because they were nerds, but mostly because she hated how much her mother compared her and her sister to them. Her brewing anger towards her mother sought an outlet.

It was a winter's day when Greta felt particularly angry. They were walking home for lunch when she began to harass the boys with name calling. They were probably taught not to fight with girls because Greta couldn't get a rise out of them. She began throwing snowballs at them because they ignored her taunts. Their lack of retaliation made her angrier and she advanced to kicking. They still wouldn't fight back! They defensively blocked her blows. Finally, she snatched their toques and tossed them into an empty corner lot where the snow was very deep. At that, the boys ran the rest of the way home to tattle.

Before she could finish two bites of her soup and sandwich, the phone rang. Myra spoke to the person on the phone in Finnish. After she hung up she turned to Greta with a stern face.

"What did you do?" she asked coarsely.

Greta didn't answer and looked down at her soup.

"That was the boys' mother! Go get their hats and bring them back now! Make sure you apologize while you're at it!" she commanded.

Pouting, Greta got up from the table and put her coat and boots back on. When she got to the empty corner lot she waded through the waist deep snow to retrieve the boys' toques. Doug and Erik's mom came to the door. Greta stood there and she offered a down-faced apology with the snow encrusted toques in her outstretched hand.

It became clear that Greta would never associate with nerdy tattle-tale boys who ran home to whine to their mother for being picked on by a girl. It all made her hate practicing piano to the point where even the subtlest inkling of pleasure from it was extinguished. The piano equated to pure mechanical drudgery.

Greta helped her dad again at the camp lot. The dock cribs were made with old railroad ties and needed to be filled with big rocks. She pulled them up from the shallow water. The bigger the better as she worked side-by-side with her father. The lumber they had harvested earlier that summer was used to build the dock. The physical activity developed a grit in her that was not typical in girls. And by the end of summer she returned to school with the determination to captain soft ball at lunch and after school.

It was always a race after lunch to see who got back to school first for sweep-scrub-wax, a fast paced version of softball with fewer players. She was eager to do track and field, running long-jump, and relay racing. She was effortlessly at the head of her class but her attention shifted towards peers who were curious about drinking, smoking, and relationships.

The boys in her class were immature and intimidated by her. She had a unique sense of style stemming from her desire to emulate her fashionista auntie. This, combined with her confident athleticism, and the ability to easily get good grades most often left her male counterparts dumbfounded. Boys her own age were into snapping girl's bras and giggling. That was the level of their flirtation and Greta met those kinds of childish antics with a steely glare, and revenge on the ball field.

The wispy white-haired child turned sandy blonde by her teens. The summer sun-kissed and streaked her hair. On hot days it took on a natural wave and once her pubescent acne subsided, her complexion glowed peachy bronze. A touch of frosted lip gloss and brown mascara on her translucent lashes were the only cosmetics she used to enhance her sapphire eyes and pleasantly plump lips.

Older boys were the only ones daring enough to strike up a conversation with Greta. She was attracted to their confidence, experience, and their desire. She was aroused during long kissing sessions; wet and wide mouths with active tongues twirling. She was assured a supply of cigarettes, pot, and booze. If they didn't have it, they knew how to get it.

Some of the parents smoked and drank, so Greta and her friends initially stole from them to get their first taste of nicotine and alcohol. The effects were powerful -- causing dizziness and nausea. There was also a sense of euphoria and loss of inhibition that Greta rebelliously enjoyed. She felt powerful, brave, adventurous and sexy when she smoked and drank. These were the activities she pursued at every opportunity.

Going from a school where she was a senior, into a high school where she was a junior opened up a whole new world for Greta where alcohol and drugs were abundant. Effortlessly, she became known as a high achiever in her grade nine math class. When they nominated her for student council she felt the familiar pressure and gnawing expectation to succeed. The voice of her mother grinded repeatedly in her head.

"Where's the other 5%?" she heard in her mind.

Overwhelmed, she declined the nomination and never mentioned it to her family.

She was drawn to non-conformists. They were the smoking area crowd who hung out at the back doors of the school between classes. The corner store across from the school sold cigarettes to anyone. They didn't strictly enforce an age limit and even sold them to young kids for their parents if they presented a handwritten note. Greta learned to forge her mother's signature and began to write her own sick notes for school when she played hooky.

Once she got to know a few of the people who smoked, they would stand around together in gaggles, bumming cigarettes and drags from one another. If anyone was broke or without, they shared within the group. It wasn't long before someone had picked up the marijuana habit and it opened the door to another level of social and psychological experiences. The effects of pot were ethereal and more interesting to Greta than boys. But boys were the way to get drugs.

Dressing for school could be challenging. She laid on the bed to get her skintight jeans zipped up. With a clingy sweater over a sheer bra, she was a hot chick and felt the stares. Sometimes she pulled together a sophisticated look that had some students looking twice to see if she was perhaps a new teacher. Her transformation made her unrecognizable. Her hair was up, glamour makeup was applied, mature pumps pinched her feet, and she wore a skirt suit handcrafted by herself. The extreme makeover managed to garner a comment from one of her teachers that she was like a chameleon. She was flattered to be praised by someone not her mother. The mother whose twisted comments never failed to let her down.

Sewing a new garment often kept her up into the wee hours especially if she wanted to wear it the next day. Everything Aunt Esther taught her about sewing laid the foundation for her to work with scissors in her hand. Working with fabric and operating the sewing machine became like second nature. Invisible hand stitching was her private perfection to please herself and onlookers. She had found a passion that wasn't driven by her mother's expectations. The sewing machine was near her bedroom and she wouldn't let herself fall asleep until the task at hand was done. The obsession to complete a new garment for the next day could take her to the brink of exhaustion.

Greta became increasingly aware of her image and sense of style. The halls and smoking area became the stage for her creations. She didn't like homogenous, off-the-rack clothing and her mother fully supported her fabric shopping sprees, maybe because she was a seamstress when she first left home. Greta took it to the next level, tackling even the most complex patterns with perfection and fine finishes. No praise forthcoming from her mother, she found it in the real world.

She had spent hours on her hair and make-up before school every morning. As soon as she was out of sight of the house, she lit a cigarette. Her wardrobe had been carefully selected the night before but ended up on the floor after several changes. Everything about her appearance was done with intent. That day in the smoking area Greta asked Jeff how she could buy a joint. He had smoked them with her in the past and told her who to go to. So at lunch time she looked for a paunchy reddish-brown haired guy with scruffy facial hair. She found the guy fitting that description wearing a plaid shirt and fringed leather vest. He was standing like a lone wolf in a corner of the smoking area. He leaned casually against the brick wall with one leg bent, smoking a cigarette as Greta approached him nervously.

"Are you Chris?" she asked.

"Who's asking?" he asked in return.

She watched him coolly take a long drag off of his cigarette as it fizzled down to the filter. He exhaled and dropped the butt to the ground, stomping it with his boot.

"I'm Greta. Jeff told me you might be able to help me out," she replied.

"Maybe I can. What do you need?" he asked.

Greta told him she wanted a joint and he gave her the price for one, or a deal for three. So she bought three and tucked them carefully in her purse. Then she found a bathroom and got in a stall where she put them in her cigarette package to keep them from getting crushed. She felt both nervous and excited to have her own pot.

After school, Greta served her father dinner and he asked for a double shot in his screwdriver that night. She practiced the piano minimally and didn't look at her homework. Instead, she watched tv and talked to Brenda on the phone. Then she went for a bike ride so she could sneak away to smoke a cigarette. There was always the chance she might meet up with friends. She smoked while she rode on the rural roads and through the many paths that cut through the wooded and bush areas.

She came upon Jeff and Mark in the woods, their bicycles on the ground. She stopped and joined in the conversation. To their surprise, she pulled out a joint and they were visibly impressed. When it was finished, Mark pulled one out and they all got good and stoned. They stood around smoking cigarettes and laughing at the dumbest things, like the shape of the clouds and the geography teacher's laser breath. Mark blew smoke rings and they tried to do the same. Then the boys rode with Greta until they got close to her home. Without a doubt, she was one of them now. They giggled, laughed, stared at each other and smoked more cigarettes. When they were still a good distance from Greta's driveway they all said good night as it was after dark. It was a school night.

Chapter 3
Peering Eyes of Nosy Neighbors

Greta's grades started slipping but she could still get passing marks without effort. It felt good not to be top of the class anymore. There were hundreds of students in her grade now and thousands in her new school. High school was exponentially larger than the elementary school she left behind.

Here, she could either stand out or blend in as much as needed. She made new friends and didn't hang out with anyone from her past anymore. Even she and Sasha had drifted apart and had none of the same classes together.

The first school dance was coming up and her new best friend, Brenda, decided to go stag. They had been asked by boys they weren't interested in. So rather than go with unsatisfactory dead weight, they agreed it would be more fun to go together. It was a Friday night in September and after dinner Brenda headed over to Greta's house so they could get ready for the dance. Brenda brought a thermos filled with alcohol she had stolen from her parents liquor cabinet. It smelled awful and tasted worse than it smelled.

"What's in this?" Greta asked with a cringe.

"I'm not sure. A little bit of everything. I didn't want it to look obvious so I poured a little from each bottle," Brenda explained.

"I'll go get some Kool-Aid to make it taste better," said Greta.

She returned with two tall glasses of red Kool-Aid with ice for them to dilute the mystery alcoholic concoction. After a few sips it started to taste good.

They primped each other's hair with the curling iron and hairspray and strategically applied make-up to their eyes, cheeks, and lips. Every modification they made to their appearance had to pass the other's approval, right down to their earrings and nail polish. This went on for nearly three hours as the girls got giddy. Finally, they were ready to walk to the school dance.

Meanwhile, Greta's dad was having a beer while dozing off in the recliner in front of the large floor model tv. She lightly nudged him.

"I'm going to the dance now with Brenda," she whispered in his ear.

"You need some money?" he asked.

"Yes please," replied Greta.

He reached into the pocket of his work pants and pulled out a money clip with folded bills. He peeled off a twenty and gave it to her.

"Do you need a ride?" he asked.

"No, we're gonna walk," Greta replied as she kissed him on the forehead.

"Ok, call me if you need a ride home," he said.

Brenda was a little taller, a little thicker, and definitely bustier than Greta. She had auburn hair and brown eyes. They toned down the freckles across her nose with a thin layer of foundation. As two strikingly different girls, they had one mission in common that night, to have a good time at all costs. Their tickets were bought in advance so the twenty bucks from Greta's dad was mad money.

Having polished off most of the liquor from the thermos, Greta and Brenda were ready to dance the night away under the strobe lights in the high school cafeteria. The DJ spun a mix of pop, disco, and rock. They ran into Chris who offered them both a hit of acid.

"Just let it dissolve under your tongue," he said.

After that, Greta lost track of Brenda. At one point it felt like the room was spinning. She slid down the wall of the cafeteria. The lights were dancing through a sea of legs as the music and voices garbled together. She was trapped in a chaotic sensory onslaught. Before fully regaining her equilibrium she pushed herself up off the floor and wobbled through the crowd until she found a crammed, smoke-filled bathroom. Girls were smoking, drinking, and throwing up in the stalls.

Spellbound by her reflection, Greta freshened up her lipstick and mascara. Her hair was perfectly tousled and flowed past her shoulders. It was the first time she saw herself as sultry and seductive puckering her lips in the mirror.

" There you are!" exclaimed Brenda. "Come on, Jeff and Mark are here."

She dragged Greta by the arm, pulling her away from her reflection.

"Let's go!" she insisted.

They wove their way through the mass and found Jeff and Mark outside. The moon was almost full and the sky was clear and starry. Klatches of people huddled like they did in the smoking area. The difference was that they were passing around mickeys of alcohol and joints, not just cigarettes. Greta didn't care that the contents of the bottle she put to her lips tasted awful. When it was her turn she swigged a large mouthful and passed it to Brenda, who did the same. The dance was ending now so the four of them walked along laughing, smoking, and drinking.

Mark said, "My parents are gone to camp so we can go to my place."

When they got there, Mark started making moves on Brenda.

"I'm going home. Are you coming?" Greta interrupted.

"No. I'm staying. You go ahead," Brenda replied and continued necking with Mark.

"I'll walk you home," Jeff said to Greta.

"Are you sure Brenda?" Greta asked again.

"Yeah. Yeah. Go ahead," she replied as Mark's hand felt Brenda's breast.

The walk in the fresh air did Greta good. Jeff accompanied her to the end of her driveway. It was dark and the driveway was long. The outside light had not been left on for her. She was heavily intoxicated and cautiously quiet. There was a key hidden on a nail under the steps. Once she got inside, she slunk to her basement bedroom and crawled under the covers as the room spun. She felt sick and hurled into a waste basket, rolled back under the covers, and passed out.

Too soon, the morning light seeped through her light coloured curtains and with squinting eyes she slowly sat up and threw up again. The smell of liquored vomit permeated the room and her pasty mouth called for something sweet and wet.

As she made her way upstairs to the refrigerator, just the motion of walking made her head throb, but she had to pull herself together in front of her parents. Patrick was gone to work. Billy had left for a ball game and Jesse was eating pancakes.

"What time did you get home?" her mom asked flatly.

"Oh... somewhere around midnight," Greta replied as she cleared her throat.

Looking disheveled, she hunched into the fridge and pulled out a carton of orange juice, placing it on the counter. Just then her dad entered the room.

"Look at me," he said.

Greta turned with her mouth half open.

"Your mother was up 'til one o'clock waiting for you and you still weren't home. So don't you lie!" he said.

Red rage grew upon her father's face.

"I won't have you embarrassing this family staying out all hours of the night!" he yelled.

Greta quickly drank a large glass of orange juice and tried to walk away.

"Look at me when I'm talking to you!" he yelled as he grabbed her arm with his big burly hand.

"Let go," said Greta, as she tried unsuccessfully to pull away.

He grabbed her by the neck the way he did when he put Patrick up against the wall.

"Don't you dare hit that girl!!" Myra yelled with authority.

At that, Sullo let his daughter go and left the house slamming the door behind him.

"Go clean yourself up. You have to babysit this afternoon for the Wilson's. They have a wedding to go to and I don't want you going over there looking like that. You smell like booze," said Myra.

From then on, Greta knew that her mother would never let her dad lay a hand on her and she could get away with just about anything.

Sullo got in his beat up old pick-up truck, leaving a trail of dust as he tore up the driveway. His usual cohort of rabble rousers were always ready to sling a few and he didn't come home that night. Myra didn't wait up.

While she was making breakfast the next morning, her husband came walking down the driveway with his head hung low and his shoulders slumped. He had crashed his truck in a ditch. He came into the house and remorsefully put an arm around Myra.   "That's it. I'm done," he said.

He swore off drinking again.

The previous day, after hydrating with more orange juice and water, Greta went to the Wilson's so they could go to their friend's wedding. Little Timothy had been fed, bathed, and freshly diapered, so she decided to take him for a walk in his stroller. This gave Greta a chance to smoke a cigarette once she was away from the peering eyes of nosey neighbours. After the walk, she put little Timothy down for a nap in his playpen and fell asleep on the couch beside him. She woke to the sound of the key in the door. She scooped up the baby who was quietly playing in his pen and propped him on her hip.

"Oh, I hope he wasn't too much trouble," said Janet Wilson.

"He was no trouble at all Mrs. Wilson. I took him for a walk and then he had a nap," Greta replied.

"We'd like to go to the reception later if you could watch Timothy again tonight," said Jonathan Wilson.

"Sure. What time do you want me here?" she asked, looking forward to the money.

"7:30 would be good. He'll be almost ready for bed by then," said Janet.

Greta called Brenda when she got home. She had spent the night at Mark's and her alibi for having been out all night was that she had slept over at Greta's. This became a recurring theme to their weekends throughout high school. They gained a lot of experience in smoking, drinking, eluding, and lying to their parents. There was always some sort of deception or plot going on for the next party.

By senior year, kids were expected to apply for college. Lots of boys, like Patrick, went straight to work in the local factory or found labour jobs. He had been desperate to get away from his abusive father for a long time and never forgave him for crashing his new motorcycle. Their dad was particularly violent after a few beers and often took it out on a non-compliant Patrick. He couldn't be perfect in his father's eyes, just as Greta couldn't be perfect in her mother's eyes. So the first chance Patrick got to take a job at the factory, he moved out.

Billy on the other hand, was small and wiry, and found ways to mostly stay out of their father's way. He avoided trouble by avoiding him. He was smart and went out of town for technical college and never came back except for Christmas. That left just Greta and Jesse at home. Greta brought home all kinds of college catalogues from the school guidance office at her mother's behest.

They spent weeks looking through the course offerings at various colleges. The number of courses offered was overwhelming. Greta would have loved to become an esthetician or massage therapist but private college was too expensive and that was the only place those courses were offered in the early eighties. She gravitated towards beauty and fashion, already doing all the hair and make-up for her friends and family and sewing 90% of her own wardrobe. She wanted to do something more creative and less academic. It was agreed that she would apply to a fashion design program in the big city.

Chapter 4
The Apartment

Greta and her parents took a trip to Circada one weekend to look for a student apartment near the college. After looking at several, they settled on a self-contained basement apartment in a large house within walking distance of the college. It had a kitchenette, three piece bathroom, and was partially furnished with a bed, loveseat, dresser and two stools. The student bachelor pad had a private entrance at the bottom of an exterior stairwell that abutted the driveway. Greta was excited about the cute place she would be living in while she went to fashion design school. Her life was heading in a whole new direction. Her mom gave the landlord a personal cheque for first and last month's rent and they were given a key so Greta could move in on the 1st of September. Then they made the long drive back home with good intentions.

She began organizing and packing the essentials right away. That meant toiletries, cosmetics, and wardrobe. It all fit into one large suitcase, a duffle bag, a backpack, and an oversized tote bag. A crossbody purse would keep her money, identification, and key safe on her person.

Greta's excitement turned to sadness the day she left. Her parents brought her to the bus station to see her off. She tried to hold back tears but cried when they waved good-bye. From the bus window, she waved back as she choked on her emotions. In that moment, Greta's life was set on a trajectory that would alter every hope and dream anyone ever had for her.

This was Greta's first time travelling alone. She stared out the window watching the farmhouses go by as the tears dried on her cheeks. There were cattle, crop fields, and other animals. The forests and rock formations were there before humans walked the land. The bus passed the turn off to their camp and the scenes became repetitious, oddly surreal in its nuanced similarity to the routine road trips to camp.

She thought about her parents, Brenda, Jeff, and even her sister Jesse, who were all left behind. She wanted to live up to her mother's expectations but feared a success that wasn't good enough. An unattainable perfection set defeat in Greta's mind before college started.

She nervously clutched her purse as a young man got up from the seat in front of her and walked past. He was only going to use the bathroom at the back of the bus. Multiple conversations overlapped and bubbled into a cacophony that reminded her of the time she took acid at the high school dance. Greta was brought back from this dreamlike state by the rocking of the bus pulling into the station. The driver announced the location for those who were only travelling that far. He said that the bus would refuel and add new passengers before continuing to their final destination. They would have about an hour to kill.

Greta disembarked with the others. Many of them lit cigarettes and those that were going no further waited for their luggage to be pulled from the cargo hold. She knew her suitcase and duffle bag were tucked in the back of the compartment because she was travelling to the last stop on the route. She lit a cigarette and walked towards the bus terminal. There, she got a diet cola from a vending machine and waited on a bench, people watching, until the bus was ready to be reboarded.

Showing the driver her ticket, he acknowledged remembering her.

"Go ahead," he said without looking at the ticket.

The bus was full this time and a man sat beside Greta. He smiled at her and tried to make conversation while Greta avoided making eye contact. After a while, he pulled a flask out of his jacket pocket and offered it to her. She would have loved to imbibe but found the man to be repulsive. So she said no and turned her head toward the window. Then she took a magazine out of her tote bag and pretended to read.

"Whatcha reading?" he asked.

Greta showed him the cover of the fashion magazine.

"Nice pictures," he said

"Well, there's articles too," Greta replied.

Then he put his arm on the armrest between them which made Greta feel uncomfortable and crowded. She felt queasy and scrunched herself towards the window. There was little space to create distance and she could smell his body odor and the liquor on his breath.

"Sorry, these seats are so small," he chuckled as he noticed her slide her butt closer to the window side of her seat.

"No problem," she replied. "I've got plenty of room."

"Yeah, you don't take up much room," said the stranger as a comment on her petite stature.

For the rest of the trip Greta's body was tense and her stomach was in a knot. After scouring every advertisement and article Greta put her tote between her head and the window and pretended to sleep. At last, the bus arrived at its final destination in the big city.

Greta waited until the man next to her exited the bus before getting out of her seat. The driver unloaded the cargo hold and placed its contents on the ground beside the bus. As people claimed their baggage, the crowd thinned out and the stranger was gone. Greta's suitcase and duffle bag were furthest to the back of the compartment and the last to come out. The driver placed them on the ground.

"It'll be easier for you if you grab one of those carts," he said, pointing to where they were.

Greta got a cart and the bus driver put her bags on it. She thanked him and he smiled.

She wheeled the cart over to the line-up of taxis waiting for fares in front of the depot. The driver of the closest cab waved her over and popped his trunk. Greta was relieved to get such prompt service. The driver held the door to the back seat open for her before getting behind the wheel.

"Where to?" he asked.

She gave him the address and they were off.

"You must be starting school next week," he said. "That area has a lot of student housing."

"That's right," Greta replied.

She gave him cash for the fare with a very small tip and he smiled and wished her good luck. She felt like she needed it.

Then she clumsily carried her oversized bag down the cement stairwell that led to her apartment door. The key was safely inside the zippered pocket of her purse that had been draped across her body for the whole trip. Upon entry, she was greeted by the stale smell of an empty bachelor pad. Its spartan decor evoked a hollowness that soon made Greta feel lonely. She tried to change her mood by unpacking to take her mind off the emptiness.

Crammed in between her clothes, makeup, and shoes were a few granola bars, dry soup packages, a jar of instant coffee, and a tin of coffee whitener. The kitchenette was stocked with utensils, dishes, a few pots and pans, and a kettle. She boiled some water and made a cup of instant soup while she freshened up in the bathroom with some of the many toiletries she'd brought.

In an effort to lift her gloom Greta decided to go out and familiarize herself with the neighborhood. She would look for places to buy food, do laundry, and determine the best route for walking to school. It was getting close to sunset but she decided to go anyway. One block up from her street was Main Street, where there were many shops, restaurants, and a bar called McCluskey's. The neon sign said Live Jazz Friday and Saturday.

Everything seemed so big and exciting once Greta left her tiny apartment. As she roamed the city streets she continued to clutch her crossbody purse. She found a coin wash laundromat that was open from 7 to 11 seven days a week. It was well lit and had a payphone, so she called her mother.

"Hello," her mother answered.

The operator interrupted to ask if she'd accept the collect call.

"Yes. Yes," said Myra. "I accept the charges."

"Hi mom. It's me," said Greta.

"Oh hello, you're there now?" she asked.

"Yes. Just calling to let you know I made it alright," Greta replied.

"Where are you calling from?" she asked.

"I found a laundromat with a phone," Greta replied.

"Okay dear. Write me and let me know how your first day of school goes," said her mother.

There was a sterile triteness to their brief exchange that left Greta feeling emotionally abandoned. They didn't talk about how the trip went or what was happening at the moment. Myra had learned to suppress her emotions a long time ago. Sensitivity was replaced by ego driven superficiality built on a need to look better than others. Now she could brag about her daughter being in college. Her own desires were projected onto Greta, a mere pawn for the measure of her maternal success and ability to produce successful offspring.

"I found a deli nearby too," Greta told her mom.

"That's nice. It's late now and long distance is expensive," said Myra.

"Oh. Ok, good night then," Greta replied.

"Good night and sweet dreams," Myra replied before hanging up.

She continued down the busy sidewalk where everyone seemed to be purposefully heading somewhere. Alone in a sea of people, not wanting to go back to her apartment, she decided to investigate McCluskey's. It was Tuesday night, so there was no jazz band. When she walked into the large dimly lit bar she inhaled the pungent aroma of beer stained carpet and years of cigarette smoke. A jukebox played Rhinestone Cowboy in the corner where a few people were shooting pool. A little nervous because she was underage, Greta popped into the ladies room. She applied a thick coat of lipstick and teased up her hair, layered on mascara, and practiced looking serious in the mirror. She had passed for being older many times in the pubs back home by using a driver's license she stole from Aunt Esther. She bore a striking resemblance to her aunt even though they were nearly seven years apart. People often mistook them for one another and thought they were sisters.

She turned up the collar on her blouse and tucked it smoothly into her skintight jeans, then undid a couple of buttons and adjusted her breasts to create cleavage. She lit a cigarette and confidently strutted up to the bar. Carefully perching herself on a barstool, she crossed her legs and tapped her cigarette on the closest ashtray. Pulling the ashtray closer, she rested her elbow on the bar. She casually and deliberately placed her chin on her perfectly manicured hand, showing off her long candy apple red nails. The bartender approached with a smile.

"What'll you have?" he asked.

"A screwdriver please," she replied.

The one drink that she knew so well was the first thing that came to mind. She thought about the times Billy was at the bar back home when she snuck in underage. He never tattled on her because he too started drinking at a young age.

She was still a child when she asked her mom what was wrong with Billy when she found him hugging the toilet one morning. Myra simply said he wasn't feeling well. He'd come home from high school, spin vinyl and lay on the floor listening to Alice Cooper through headphones. The song, I'm Eighteen came to mind as she would soon be turning eighteen.

The bartender returned with a cardboard coaster and Greta's drink. She hid her surprise at how expensive it was and sipped it very slowly. The longer it lasted, the longer she avoided going back to her empty apartment.

Greta sensed eyes on her through her peripheral vision. There was an old man at the far end of the bar, like a fixture, leering at her. It took her back to when she was prepubescent and an elderly man rented a small bungalow on her parent's property. One day when Greta was walking past the bungalow he handed her a magazine. He was old, fat, had missing teeth, and wore dirty clothes. His smile gave her the creeps, but she didn't want to be rude so she took the magazine.

"Thanks," she replied shyly, trying to avoid eye contact.

"I hope you like it," he replied.

Greta peeked at the cover and immediately folded the magazine under her arm. There was a naked woman spreading her legs and touching herself on the cover. Greta's heart raced and her face flushed as she scurried away.

It was a hot day, so she changed into a bikini and spread a blanket on the lawn. While laying on her stomach, tanning her back, she flipped through the pages of sexually explicit women. It was an arousing taboo that made her wary of the motives of the old man in the bungalow. She took a wide berth whenever walking past him from then on. He stood on the little wooden porch with a toothless grin and squinty eyes. About a week had passed.

"Did you like the magazine?" he beckoned to her.

She was mute and briskly kept going.

Greta watched the ice cubes melt in the bottom of her glass. Then the bartender placed another screwdriver in front of her.

"From the gentleman at the end of the bar," he said.

With a lump in her throat she smiled at the man at the end of the bar and nodded. He raised his glass to her. She was glad to have a fresh drink and pulled out another cigarette. From her right came a hand with a lighter.

"Let me get that for you," said a young man with wavy brown hair that looked like it was about a month overdue for a cut.

A sense of relief filled Greta. She leaned towards the lighter as he flicked it.

"Thanks," she said as the ember glowed.

"Let me introduce myself. I'm Cory," said the handsome stranger.

"Pleased to meet you. I'm Greta," she replied, extending her beautifully manicured hand.

"My friend Graham and I were wondering... If you're alone, maybe you'd like to join us," he said as he pointed to a small round table near the pool tables.

His friend waved.

Feeling like she'd been rescued from the leering eyes of the old man, Greta slid off the bar stool and joined the young men. Graham stood up and introduced himself as he pulled a chair out for Greta. When the waitress came over, he ordered a second pitcher of draft with an extra glass for Greta. The rest of her screwdriver was done by the time the waitress returned and Greta immediately joined in with her new cohorts on the amber brew.

After a few glasses and a trip to the bathroom, Greta realized she was getting wobbly and needed to think about getting back to her apartment.

"Guys, I have to get going. It's getting late," she told them.

"Awe, come on," whined Graham. "Just one more."

He refilled her glass with tepid draft. Another cigarette subdued its raunchiness.

"Ok guys, I really gotta go. But maybe I'll see you around again sometime," she said as she got up to leave.

"It was nice meeting you," said Cory, giving her a warm hug.

"Nice to meet you too," she replied.

"We're here a couple nights a week. Hope to see you again soon," he added.

Greta got her bearings and turned right on Main Street. The alley she used earlier when it was still daylight had become dark and shadowy. The trees and buildings were moving. It was eerie, but the shortest route to her apartment. She walked quietly and was alert to every sound. She peeked over her shoulder to make sure she wasn't being followed and clutched her purse tightly. Pulling out her key, she held it firmly, with the point jutting out between her fingers. Her heart jumped as a cat screeched and ran past her. Halfway down the alley there was an abandoned dumpster laying on it's side where several feral cats were hanging out. She picked up her pace, thinking they might be aggressive and anxiously made it to a streetlight. Then she heard footsteps. There was nothing she could see over her shoulder. Maybe she was just imagining it in her drunken stupor. The unfamiliar territory and shadows could have been playing tricks on her.

Once she made it safely to her apartment, she locked herself in. She fell onto her bed without removing her clothes and passed out until morning.

Chapter 5
Coffee, Cigarettes, and Dry Ramen

Hung over, Greta opened her eyes in a state of disorientation. She got up and dug in her suitcase in search of her watch and clock radio. Her watch said two and she knew it was afternoon because of the daylight peeking through the curtains. She set up her clock radio and put the kettle on to make an instant coffee. Then she started a bubble bath, adding a couple of kettles of boiled water to make the tub water hotter.

She was used to having saunas all of her life. In fact, her father and his eight siblings were all born in a sauna as was customary back in the old country. Traditionally, they built the sauna before building the home. That's how central the sauna was to their culture.

She found a radio station, put her coffee cup on the side of the tub and slowly immersed herself into the scalding hot suds. The coffee was helping lift the hangover fog. She submerged her long sandy blonde hair and applied a palmful of vanilla scented shampoo. As the lather sat on her hair she worked a bar of soap over her supple limbs. She closed her eyes and allowed the tension in her muscles to melt away. Sweat poured from her brow as she felt herself detoxifying. She was repulsed by the old man who bought her the screwdriver and how he reminded her of the one who gave her the dirty magazine.

Greta stepped out of the tub and patted her body gently with a towel before squeezing her hair. Warm and pink skinned, she looked at herself in the full length mirror behind the bathroom door. As steam wafted out of the bathroom Greta's reflection became clearer. Her stomach was concave and her waist was narrow. She sucked in her stomach and looked at her body from all angles. She would have looked unhealthy if it weren't for the roundness of her breasts and buttocks. She hated her thick thighs and stood on her tippy toes to lengthen her leg. Better, she thought.
Proud of herself for not having eaten anything since the instant soup the day before, she made another instant coffee and treated herself to a granola bar. She felt guilty if she ate too much and often smoked to suppress her appetite.

She turned up the radio and in her bra and panties did the Jane Fonda's workout she knew from memory. A couple of Christmases ago, her mother gifted her with the book. As a dutiful daughter, Greta set the exercises to task and memorized them. The routine became a daily practice akin to the discipline of piano. She even did it in the living room while her mother watched from the kitchen. However, no matter how many times she did the routine over months and years, she could never attain the ideal look of Jane Fonda's body portrayed on the front cover of her book. Greta's short stature was in stark contrast to Fonda's long slender build.

After twisting, bouncing, and contorting her body Greta stretched out on her bed with a towel under her still damp hair. Her first day of school would be Monday and it was only Wednesday. So she finished unpacking, hung her clothes, and ironed the ones that had become wrinkled, compulsively pairing pieces to make outfits.

Over the next few days Greta didn't eat much. No matter how beautiful she was she obsessed about the tiniest perceived imperfections in her appearance. She wasn't tall enough, her teeth weren't straight enough, her thighs and calves were too thick and her feet were too big. She had worn braces and her dentist told her she could be in a toothpaste commercial. All she could see was a distorted face when she smiled. Afraid that her cheeks looked chubby, she self-consciously forced sullenness.

Greta made sure she could afford cigarettes by buying cheap bulky foods like oatmeal, rice, and dry ramen. Coffee and cigarettes took away her hunger pangs and allowed her waist to stay small. And since she walked everywhere and did the Fonda workout, her body quickly burned off the few calories she consumed. Greta watched everything she ate.

Her mother had been fat. Myra put on more weight after each child and when she lost her figure she began to hate herself. Then she joined Weight Watchers and became obsessed with counting calories and recording everything she ate. She took long walks and recorded how far and how long she walked. Soon she was watching everything that Greta put in her mouth too and told her how many calories each morsel contained.

Myra measured her own bust, waist, and hips, and weighed herself every morning. Dress size was a highly significant figure. Greta began to think that even her shoe size was too big so she squeezed into shoes too small for her to satisfy her mother. She wasn't good enough just the way she was. Like coming home with an A without the plus.

``How does the small fit?" Myra asked from outside the fitting room. "Let me see."

More words in her mother's voice stuck in Greta's head.

Greta opened the fitting room curtain and stepped out, sucking herself in. Feeling like she was about to bust a seam, her mother inspected her as she looked at herself in the mirror.

"Well I'm sure if you lose a couple of pounds it will fit just right. You don't want to get any bigger than that," said Myra.

She couldn't help herself sometimes. After school Greta ate an entire box of cookies with milk after having eaten nothing for twenty-four hours. She felt guilty and dreaded her skintight jeans not fitting the next day. She hated herself for gorging when no one was around. Then she'd lock herself in the bathroom where she tied her hair back and plunged a finger down her throat. She forced herself to throw up the entire contents of her stomach until she reached yellow bile. When she knew she'd got it all out, she brushed her teeth and rinsed with minty mouthwash. Once, when she got out of the bathroom, Jesse was sitting in the family room, all too quietly watching television.

"I know what you did. I could hear you. You were throwing up," Jesse said.

"I was not! And mind your own business anyway," Greta denied.

Greta was more careful after. She did this whenever she indulged and regretted it. She deliberately chose soft foods that wouldn't hurt coming back up. Binge eating and vomiting was a segue into binge drinking, intertwined with her warped obsession to achieve an unattainably perfect size and shape.

School started in the big city of Circada but Greta was not focused or mentally present in class. The books were expensive and heavy and after a couple of weeks there was no spark for the classroom. She was homesick for familiar faces.

That night, she called her old friend Jeff from the laundromat payphone. He was working at the factory and earning a steady wage, saving money by sharing an apartment with some guy. He said that Brenda was working at Mike's Lunch and was pregnant with Mark's baby. They had shacked up.

Mostly they talked about stuff back home and Greta pretended everything was fine, that being in the big city was exciting. Talking to him made her desire companionship. So she folded and bagged her laundry and dropped it off at her tiny apartment. Then she walked up the alley of cats to McCluskey's where she propped herself up on a barstool.

"A glass of draft please," she said to the bartender.

"No screwdriver tonight?" he asked, remembering the petite blonde with red lips, tight jeans, and a sullen smile.

"Not tonight. Just a draft thanks," she replied, realizing her budget.

The live jazz band was on and it was sublimely hypnotic. The bar was filling up and someone sat beside her. She only subtly glanced and saw a rough looking man with a five o'clock shadow and long straight dirty blonde hair. He wore black jeans and a black leather vest over a paisley patterned dress shirt. He butted his cigarette out in the ashtray closest to Greta.

"Excuse me," he said.

"No problem," Greta replied as his strong cologne wafted in her direction.

The bartender came to take his order.

"A rum and coke. And whatever the lady wants," he said.

"I'll have what he's having, thanks," she replied.

They clinked glasses when their drinks arrived and he couldn't help but be struck by her clear blue eyes.

"I'm Daryl by the way," he introduced himself.

His roughness was somehow dangerously attractive and aroused Greta's desire to be rebellious, against her mother, against school, against perfection, and against the need to conform to social constructs.

"I'm Greta," she smiled softly.

"There's an empty table over there," he said. "Wanna grab it before someone else does?"

"Sure," she replied.

He was interested in everything she said about her hometown and how she hated school and wanted to quit and just get a job. He kept buying her drinks as quickly as she could finish them. Daryl asked Greta if she liked pot and he said he had some back at his apartment. So they finished what they were drinking and got into his dark tinted car.

"It's not far," he said.

Greta was quite drunk and looked forward to smoking some weed since she hadn't had any since back home with Brenda and the guys. They pulled into the back lane of an old house and got out of the car. He took Greta by the hand.

"Come on, it'll only take a minute," he said.

They climbed an exterior staircase to a large second story deck on the back of the house where there was an apartment door.

"Is this your place?" Greta asked.

"My chum lives here. He owes me some," Daryl replied.

He knocked. There was no answer. The apartment looked dark and silent as if no one was home but Daryl kept knocking harder and harder.

"Fuck!" he exclaimed.

Then he pushed on the window. It wouldn't open. Greta was getting scared and moved towards the stairs while Daryl's back was turned.

"Where do you think you're going?!" he turned and yelled.

He rushed at her and grabbed her by the arm.

"We're waiting until he gets back," he said.

"I really think I should go," she replied.

"We're waiting!" he said harshly, blocking the stairs.

She was trapped by this guy and didn't know what bad things he had in mind for her. She needed to think smart, sobered up quickly, and said nor did anything to anger him further.

"Ok, well then let's have a smoke," she complied calmly as she pulled out two cigarettes, offering him one.

They both smoked as Daryl's posture loosened up with the nicotine infusion. He started mumbling and pacing. He made no sense as she assessed the surroundings. There was a clothesline from the deck to a pole at the far corner of the back yard. When his back was turned, Greta grabbed the line and swung down to the ground, breaking a heel on the landing. Her hands and knees were scraped but she had no time to feel pain. She got up quickly and ran to the nearest neighbor. Pounding on their back door she could hear Daryl's fury!

"You little bitch!" he screamed.

The lights came on and a man holding a baseball bat came to the door. He was tying up his bathrobe as Greta cried out.

"Someone is trying to kidnap me," she pleaded. "Please help me."

The man let her in and his wife came and invited her to sit at their kitchen table.

"We should call the police," said the wife.

"No. I'll be fine. I just want to go home," said Greta.

"Can we call someone? Your parents?" the woman asked.

"No. I'm not from around here. I have an apartment near the college though," she replied. "I don't know my way around. Can I take a bus from here?"

"It's too dangerous to be out this late alone," said the man.

The woman ran some cool water on a towel and wiped the dirt off of Greta's badly scraped hands.

"We'll give you a ride home," he said. "There's always some shady goings-ons happening over there."

As the kind couple escorted Greta to their car, there was no sign of Daryl although his car was still parked in the back.

"Which college are you near?" asked the husband.

"George Brown. But if you know McCluskey's I'm one block south of there," she replied.

"Yeah. I know exactly where that is," he replied.

They dropped her off at her driveway and wished her well.   "I can't thank you enough," she said.

"No need dear. We're just glad you're ok," said the wife.

Disheveled and stunned by what she'd just been through, Greta tossed and turned for hours. She dreamt that there was a dark figure in her open doorway. Someone was in her apartment watching her sleep. When she woke, she swore it was real but couldn't be sure that it wasn't a dream. That Saturday and Sunday, she didn't leave her apartment.

Chapter 6
A Carrot Muffin and Thick Thighs

On her way to school on Monday, Greta had a change of plans. She bought a newspaper and found a coffee shop to sit in. Joe's Coffee House was a quaint mom and pop style diner with a long sit-down counter with red vinyl topped stools. There was a middle section with tables and chairs that had matching red vinyl upholstery, and the booths were adjacent to the big front windows that looked out onto the sidewalk of Main Street. Each booth had its own individual coin operated miniature jukebox, and a big floor model jukebox sat at the back of the restaurant near the payphone and public washrooms. With a pen in hand Greta began looking through the help wanted ads.

The waitress approached and refilled her coffee before it got to the bottom. She was a mature woman in nursing shoes.

"Can I warm that up for you dear?" she asked.

"Yes please," Greta replied as she briefly lifted her eyes from the paper.

"Can I get you something to eat?" asked the waitress. It said Connie on her nametag which was neatly pinned to the strap of the white apron that was part of her snug dusty rose uniform. Her hair was flawlessly coiffed and pulled up off her neck with curls arranged and pinned on the top of her head. She wore too much makeup but could get away with it. The beauty of her youth was still evident.

Greta was hungry but didn't want to eat and didn't want to spend money on food.

"No thanks," she replied.

After Connie had made her rounds she came back with a muffin on a small plate and placed it in front of Greta.

"You look like you could use a little something. It's carrot, from yesterday, but it's still good. On the house," said Connie with a gentle smile.

"Thank you so much," Greta beamed.

She pinched off a piece of the muffin and popped it in her mouth. It dissolved with a sip of coffee. She circled a couple of ads that specified to apply in person and when Connie returned with the cheque for Greta's coffee she noticed the circled ads.

"One of our girls just quit yesterday and we need someone two nights a week," said the mature waitress.

Greta's face lit up and her posture straightened.

"Really? How do I apply?" Greta asked.

"The boss is working in the kitchen right now. I'll go see if he's got time to talk to you. If you're interested that is," said Connie.

"Oh Yes. Yes. I'm interested. That would be great," said Greta, with the biggest smile since arriving in the big city.

Greta watched Connie walk back to the kitchen and saw her talking to the boss through the food service window. Their conversation was brief. She saw Connie point to Greta as they looked in her direction. Greta straightened up with a tightlipped smile. Then Connie and the boss came out of the kitchen. He went and sat at the last booth in the back corner of the dining room with his back to the wall. Connie walked back to Greta.

"He'll see you now," she said.

Greta nervously sat down across from the boss. She noticed the tip of one of his index fingers was missing. Maybe he cut it in a kitchen accident. It reminded her of her father's thumb that was sawed off in a work accident when Greta was young. The doctor's were able to rebuild a functional and sensate replacement through a series of operations.

Part of the procedure to rebuild her father's thumb involved removing a piece of shin bone to replace what was lost in the accident. A nerve from an adjacent finger was fed over to the new thumb to give it feeling. New skin and tissue were grafted by attaching the appendage that was being rebuilt to her father's abdomen skin. There were months of rehabilitation but the new thumb worked. It was missing a joint and thumbnail and was sensitive to the cold.

During his recovery, Patrick came home very drunk one night and an argument ensued between father and son. Patrick pushed Sullo. His already compromised leg broke in the fall, in the place where bone had been removed for his new thumb. There was screaming and Myra called an ambulance. It was the last straw, the last physical altercation between them. With his father in the hospital, Patrick moved out the next day. It would be decades before they spoke to one another again.

"So you're looking for a job," the boss said bluntly.

Greta took a deep breath and carefully answered.

"Yes sir. I am."

"Have you ever waitressed before?" he asked.

"I used to serve at wedding banquets back home," said Greta enthusiastically. "So I know how to carry trays and pour coffee, and I'm a quick learner too."

"Well I need someone to start immediately, tomorrow afternoon. You will have to learn from the other girls," said the boss.

"That's fine," she replied. "I know I can do it."

"Ok, I'll give you a try," he said. "I'm Joe. You can go to the back room and find a uniform that fits. Be here fifteen minutes before your shift starts tomorrow at 2."

Greta stood up and thanked Joe. She smiled at Connie who glanced over from the customer she was serving. Then Greta followed Joe to the back room where she looked over the uniforms that were hanging on a rack.

"Find one that fits and be on time tomorrow ready to work," he said.

"I will. Thank you very much," replied Greta.

After finding a small uniform she went back out to the dining room and stood in front of the cash register at the end of the counter. Connie came to the cash.

"Staff doesn't pay for coffee. Go on now," she said.

"That's great," she beamed. "You have no idea how much I appreciate this."

"See you tomorrow hon," Connie replied as Greta turned and walked away.

With this new injection of confidence, Greta was up on her toes as she strutted in the direction of Young Street to look for the addresses that she'd circled in the newspaper. She knew she would have to tell her mother that she was quitting school and the only way she could do that was if she had a job. Two days a week was not enough.

She took a deep breath and became aware of her surroundings. The density of people increased once she got to Young Street. There were people from all walks of life. The diversity of the population was obvious to a girl who had grown up in a mostly white northern town. It was exhilarating.

Crossing the street on the flashing walk signal, Greta saw the sign for Jeans N Tops. It was one of the stores she had circled in the newspaper. She went in and said she was interested in applying for the job. They gave her an application form to fill out but she didn't have a home phone. There were no cell phones in the early eighties so she asked if she could borrow a phone book to look up the number for Joe's Coffee House. She used their phone number and wrote work number beside it.

She went to two more stores in the area that were looking for sales help and left applications with them also. She was feeling hopeful and excited as she walked back home. If you could call it home, the tiny bachelor apartment.

She took the uniform out of the plastic bag. It was wrinkled and smelled funny so she soaked it in the sink with a little dish detergent and scrubbed the armpits and dingy areas with a bar of soap. After letting it soak she gave it several good rinses in cool water until it looked and smelled fresh. Then she squeezed out as much water as she could by hand and hung it over the shower curtain rod to drip dry.

She made a cup of instant coffee and prepared a hot bath with a couple of pots of boiled water added to it. Then she slowly stepped in, letting her skin adjust to the heat. She laid back and looked at her floating breasts covered in bubbles.

The perspiration rolled down her face as she took a face cloth and wiped away her makeup. She poured some baby oil on the warm cloth to remove the layers of mascara from her lashes. She soaped up the cloth and rubbed it over her entire body, from her shoulders to her breasts, stomach, buttocks, down to her feet.

Then she stood up, drained the tub, lathered her hair with vanilla shampoo and turned on the shower to rinse herself completely. The clean water streamed over her pink body as she touched her privates. There was a flutter in her pelvis. She turned off the water and stepped on a pile of clothes on the floor. Dripping, she rubbed herself vigorously. She wiped away the steam from the mirror on the bathroom door and turned sideways. Leaning against the vanity, she imagined being watched. Her pretend voyeur was aroused and she opened her mouth wide. Her eyes closed, and her back arched as she frantically rubbed herself. Juices oozed from within her as they provided lubrication and pulsating waves of endorphins flooded her body. She lingered in the moment as the euphoria slowly subsided, reminded by her reflection that her thighs were too thick.

She began to miss Jeff again and wrote a scintillating letter to him that she would mail on her way to work. She wrote a letter to her mother too but tore it up. Then she set the alarm on her clock radio, ate a bowl of ramen noodles, laid down and fell asleep peacefully.

The next morning, Greta began her day by making an instant coffee and doing Jane Fonda to the radio. She spent a couple of hours curling her hair, teasing and spraying it. During that time, she applied a base layer of foundation to her face. She rouged her cheeks lightly, applied a frosty gloss over her naturally pink lips and coated her translucent lashes with a brown mascara.

Her uniform had dried well, so she ironed it and carefully folded it into a tote where she had already placed a pair of beige strappy wedge sandals. She gathered up the textbooks she had purchased for college and put them in her backpack. It was already early afternoon so she quickly slipped on a pair of flip flops, put the heavy backpack on, and gathered her necessities. Locking the door as she left, she placed her key in the zipper pocket of her crossbody purse.

Greta was running low on cash. It was near the end of the month and the college allowance from her mother was almost depleted. She needed to return the textbooks for cash. Once she'd done that, she had enough money to last until the next cheque arrived. However, she wouldn't tell her mother that she quit school until after getting the cheque.

First off, she bought a diet coke and a pack of cigarettes. She sat down on a park bench and tried to rationalize her premeditated deceit. It was a path to freedom. She was breaking free from living up to her mother's expectations. She needed more time to prove her independence. They were all lies and excuses for her failure. She told herself she just needed the money to survive until she could make it on her own. She gradually pushed the contentious thoughts out of her mind with each drag and distracted herself with people-watching. Everyone was going somewhere and looked like they had their lives together, but Greta didn't know where she was going in life. Her future was uncharted now that she had committed to going it alone.

Greta got up slowly, straightened out her blouse and flipped her bouncy curls off of her shoulders before heading up Young Street towards Main. She shook out the cobwebs as she ambled and looked at the shop windows. She noticed a help wanted sign at a dry cleaner's. She had plenty of time before work, so she stepped into the shop where she was greeted by an elderly woman with an accent.

"How can I help you?" the woman asked succinctly.

"I saw the help wanted sign in your window," Greta replied.

"You work in laundry before?" asked the woman with a strong accent.

"No. But I can learn," said Greta.

"Here, fill this out," the woman barked as she handed her a clip board with an application form and pen.

The woman turned around and went back to sorting laundry. Greta had memorized the phone number at Joe's Coffee House from having filled out the application at Jeans N Tops. She was neat and thorough and gave Joe's phone number as her contact.

"I'm finished," Greta said loudly, trying to get the woman's attention.

The woman walked over to the counter, put her head down and quickly scanned over the application.

"I call you here?" she asked, pointing at the number for Joe's.

"Yes. If I am not there just leave a message. I don't have a home phone number yet. That's where I work, part-time," Greta answered.

"Ok. Ok. I need full-time!" the lady replied, frankly.

Then the woman folded the application form into a square and tucked it into her smock pocket as she turned back to her work.

Greta left the humid dry cleaner's feeling like her hair had dropped an inch.

Chapter 7
The Bells Chimed

Greta arrived early at Joe's Coffee House. Joe the boss was in the kitchen and Connie was carrying food to one of the booths. Carrying a plate on her right forearm and another plate in her right hand, Connie placed the coffee pot from her left hand on the table. Then she took the plate from her forearm and placed it in front of the lady to her left. At the same time, she put the plate in her right hand in front of the man to her right. She did this with automated fluidity. Then she topped-up their coffees, exchanged a few words and went along from table to table pouring coffee and removing dirty dishes. All the while, Connie made time to lift her head and smile at Greta as she walked past.

She made the job look easy, and Greta was more than a little nervous and intimidated. Feeling flushed, she entered the staff washroom and changed into her uniform which managed to stay relatively wrinkle free. She powdered her face and applied another layer of mascara and lipstick before taking a deep breath. Her strappy wedge sandals added an extra two and a half inches to her height. She cinched the loose fitting uniform snuggly behind her back with the apron that went over top of it. Then she reported to Joe in the kitchen.

He yelled, waving his hands, "You need to tie your hair up! Put a net on it or something! You can't have it hanging over the food like that!"

Greta shrunk and meekly replied, "Ok."

She immediately searched out Connie and found her cashing out a customer.

"Keep the change Connie," said the customer in a familiar tone.

"Thanks Tim. See ya tomorrow," Connie answered back.

"Hi hon," she said as she noticed Greta's draped locks.

Greta was visibly nervous and felt like she was interrupting. She explained her hair situation to Connie.

"Relax hon. There's a bunch of extra elastics and bobby pins in the staff washroom behind the mirror. Just help yourself," she told her.

Greta went back to the washroom and found hairnets, and a wide assortment of elastics and pins behind the vanity mirror. After she corrected her hair faux pas with a scrunchy and some bobby pins she reported back to Connie for approval. Connie gave her a thumbs up and told her to take a tray and observe for a few minutes.

"I'm only here until six to help train you," said Connie. "Then you'll be working with Darlene until closing."

Greta watched Connie very carefully, studied the menu, and put a pen and pad in her apron. She familiarized herself with where everything was located. The cutlery, condiments, coffee machine, dessert fridge, there was just so much of it. Dirty dishes were placed on the cart in a tray by the kitchen door for the kitchen staff. Food orders were placed on the service window shelf and called out to Joe who prepared the meals that he then placed on the service shelf when they were ready for pickup. Everything ran smoothly and had a definite order of operations.

"You will take the center row of tables. I'm on the counter and the booths," Connie said to Greta. "That way we won't be in each other's way while you learn."

"Ok," replied Greta.

"If you have any questions, let me know. Tips are your own," Connie explained as the bells on the door chimed. "Those people coming in are sitting at one of your tables so you can start now."

Both nervous and excited, Greta took a deep breath and walked with confidence over to her first customers. She greeted them with a smile and gave them each a menu.

"Would you like coffees?" she asked the couple.

They responded in the affirmative. Greta carefully filled their cups to below the brim, leaving enough room for creamer to be added. Utensils and everything they needed were set at the table. These were replaced and refilled as needed between customers.

"Would you like a few minutes to look at the menu? Or do you know what you'd like to order?" she asked.

They ordered on the spot as Greta jotted it on her pad. She took the order to the kitchen window.

"Western sandwich combo! Burger with the works and fries!" she called out to the kitchen staff being ruled over by Joe.

That took the initial nervousness out of Greta's system. The bells chimed again. She turned around and there were more people coming to sit in her assigned section. Connie was passing by with a fresh pot of coffee.

"Go get 'em Greta," she said with an encouraging nudge.

Greta smiled and brought menus and a coffee pot with her to her next customers. The hours flew by quickly.

Greta wiped down and reset each table in between customers. The atmosphere in the diner was simmering with many conversations, the clatter of utensils and dishes, and Joe's booming voice in charge of production and quality control.

Then someone got up and put coins in the jukebox. They flipped through the charts and pressed the buttons. On came Van Halen. Followed by Elton John, The Beatles, and ZZ Top. Food was being served up and enjoyed, and pots of coffee were being brewed one after another. At the moment, there was no place Greta would rather be than in the middle of this buzzing hive of food, conversation, and music. Everything and everyone was part of the atmosphere. From the kitchen staff and customers to the decor, music and the smell of good food all contributed to the vibe at Joe's Coffee House.

"I'm finishing up in twenty minutes hon," said Connie as she stacked a pile of dirty dishes on the cart.

Just then, Darlene entered the restaurant. She strode past briskly on her way to the staff room. She was a tall husky woman with big hands and thick ankles. She was statuesque with her short hair neatly combed and covered with a hairnet. She wore trendy black bobble earrings with a matching necklace, hot pink lipstick and canary yellow eyeshadow. She took over Connie's booths and counter seating. The transition between Connie and Darlene's shifts was smooth and natural.

Darlene approached Greta while she was getting lemon meringue pie and orange Jello from the dessert fridge.

"I'm Darlene by the way," she said in a deep but soft voice.

Greta smiled brightly and replied, "Nice to meet you. I'm Greta."

"Nice to meet you too," said Darlene.

They went back to serving tables, passing each other throughout the evening. Darlene checked in with Greta periodically to see how she was doing. Greta marveled at Darlene's thoroughness and undwindling stamina. At one point they were behind the counter near the coffee machine at the same time. "You're probably gonna want to consider wearing some sneakers or something," Darlene told her.

Darlene was wearing comfortable well-padded white nursing shoes. Greta's strappy sandals were digging into her skin and there were still two hours to go until closing time.

"I think you are right," Greta replied.

"Your shoes are adorable," Darlene added. "Don't get me wrong. They just ain't practical for this kinda work. I can see the straps digging in."

"Yup, I'll catch on and I appreciate any other tips you can give me," Greta winced. "To be honest, my feet are killing me."

"Don't worry hon, you'll get the hang of things," said Darlene. "You're doing great so far."

Greta and Darlene worked well together for the rest of the evening. The kitchen closed at nine-thirty but they still served coffee and baked goods until eleven. After the dinner rush, there was more time to restock the cutlery and condiments and do cleaning.

At ten-thirty Darlene asked Greta to start sweeping where there were no customers.

"We just have to sweep. The guys from the kitchen will come out and mop later," she said.

Ok, great," Greta replied.

Her feet were rubbed raw as she worked through her discomfort and finished sweeping. Joe emerged from the kitchen and took the receipts and money tray out of the cash register. Then he sat down at the last booth and hollered at Greta.

"Come and sit down!"

Relieved to get off of her feet, but also nervous, Greta sat across from Joe. His booming voice reminded her of her dad's and how she reacted to it out of fear.

"Darlene! Bring a piece of pie and a glass of milk!" he called out in his kitchen voice.

Darlene placed the pie and milk in front of Greta.

Joe said, "Eat!"

It wasn't until then that Greta realized she hadn't eaten anything all day. Maybe because she was famished it was the best piece of apple pie she'd had in her whole life. The glass of milk reminded her of her sister Jesse.

"You come to work same time tomorrow?" Joe asked rhetorically.

"Yes. Yes. Of course," answered Greta with her mouth full.

"I pay you next Friday. Every two weeks," said Joe.

"Ok," she gulped. "Thank you. Thank you very much."

She took another forkful of pie and washed it down with half a glass of milk. Then she remembered the other job applications.

"Oh, I applied for another job and gave them the phone number here because I don't have a phone yet," she said.

With a stern eye, Joe glanced up from the money he was counting without lifting his head.

"Ok. Business only. No personal calls," he said.

"Of course. I totally understand," she replied meekly. "And thank you again."

"Ok. You can leave. And be on time tomorrow," said Joe in a brusk tone. "With your hair up!"

After picking up her dirty dishes, Greta came back with a rag and wiped down the spot where she'd been eating.

"Can I get you anything?" she asked him sweetly.

Joe lifted his head and gave her a little smile. There was a glint in his eye.

"A coffee with cream would be nice," he said in an uncharacteristically soft tone.

When she returned, she said, "See you tomorrow."

Receiving no reply as he continued counting the cash, she went to the back room where Darlene was. She took off her sandals, revealing several red raw blisters on her feet. She was so relieved to put flip flops on.

Darlene asked her if she was ok.

"I'll be alright," Greta said.

And they left the restaurant together. Darlene locked the door with her own key.

"I'll see you tomorrow then," she said, and they went their separate ways.

Streetlights, headlights, and apartment windows illuminated the city night. Greta put her hand into her crossbody purse and pulled out her cigarette pack. She slid it open to retrieve a cigarette and matches. Putting the package back in her purse, she stopped and put the cigarette in her mouth, struck a match, and took the first puff she'd had since before work. Feeling a little lightheaded, she exhaled and put the matches in her pocket.

There was a lull in activity by this time of the evening compared to the usual daytime bustle but the city was still alive. The cool evening air relieved some of the pain in her feet and comforted her bare skin and raw blisters. She continued on Main Street and came to the alley that led to her apartment. It was filled with long shadows and Greta's nerves were set on edge. She took her key out of her purse and fit it between her knuckles, pointing out like a weapon.

She thought to herself 'surely I can stab a person in the eye with this key if I need to defend myself'.
At the end of the alley she saw two silhouettes go past. Hearing footsteps from behind, she peeked over her shoulder but saw no one. She began to walk more briskly. The flip flops slapped the ground and the bottom of her feet so that she couldn't make out any other sounds. Out of the darkness, a cat screeched past and Greta's heart skipped a beat as she ran to the sidewalk at the end of the alley. A streetlight brought everything into view as she relaxed, caught her breath, and looked back down the alley. There was the old man from McCluskey's. The one who had bought her a screwdriver. He was wearing a long overcoat.

With a leer, he slurred, "Evening miss."

Greta croaked out a hello and quickly crossed to the other side of the street towards her apartment.

"Have a good evening," he said.

Then he walked slowly and watched where she was going. As soon as he wasn't looking, she sprinted down the driveway to her apartment. Her rattled nerves had gotten the better of her.

She went straight to the bathroom, turned on the shower as hot as possible and undressed. She stepped in and stood under the water. Then she lathered up a bar of soap and ran her sudsy hands over her body. Just as she was beginning to relax, she thought she might have forgotten to lock the apartment door in her panicked state. So she rinsed off quickly and stepped out onto the pile of clothes she had left on the bathroom floor. She quickly dried off her feet, wrapped a towel on her head and tiptoed through the carpeted bachelor pad, naked, to check the door. It was locked.

She patted herself thoroughly and hung the damp towel on a hook on the back of the bathroom door. Then she closed the shower curtain so it could drip dry and went to her bed where she placed a dry towel on her pillow to rest her damp hair. There, she fell asleep in a matter of seconds.

Chapter 8
The Catwalk

Greta woke in the middle of the night. In a cold sweat she lay naked and sprawled crosswise on the disheveled bed. The bathroom light was on. She quickly went to the bathroom because she thought she'd started her period. But when she wiped herself there was a thick pasty goo. Had she had an erotic dream?

Shivering, she put on a sweatshirt and sweatpants. She was especially groggy. She crawled back into bed, buried herself under the covers and fell back to sleep.

There was a loud knock that startled Greta out of her sleep. She threw off the covers and nervously approached the door. On her tiptoes she looked through the peephole. It was her landlord who lived on the main floor of the house. When she went to open the door, she saw that it was unlocked. But she remembered checking it when she got out of the shower the night before.

Confused, she opened the door, cleared her throat and said hello.

" I hope I'm not disturbing you. I just wanted to drop off your mail," he said.

Charlie stretched to look over Greta and into the apartment. Her face was clean and her hair was tousled.

"Is everything ok?" he asked.

"Yes. Fine. Thanks," she replied as she pushed the hair off her forehead and took the two envelopes from his hand.

"Alright, let me know if you ever need anything. I'm always around," said Charlie, who lived right above Greta.

His was the front door of the house.

"Will do," said Greta.

She shut the door and locked it. She had been prone to sleepwalking as a child and wondered if she had unlocked it during the night, perhaps thinking it was the bathroom door.

Holding the envelope from her mom, Greta thought about what a disappointment she was to her. How would she go about telling her mother that she had quit school?

She opened it because she knew there would be a cheque inside, but she didn't read the enclosed letter. She put the cheque in her purse and pondered the unopened letter from Jeff. She left the unopened letter and the unread note on the counter for later.

Then she gathered up the pile of clothes from her bathroom floor. She stuffed her dirty laundry into a garbage bag and changed into a pair of jeans. She slipped her flip flops on her blistered feet, draped her purse across her body, and grabbed her laundry. Then she left and deliberately locked the door with her key.

With the garbage bag full of laundry tossed over her shoulder, Greta briskly walked through the alley which was as charming during the day as it was creepy during the night. Instead of ominous long shadows cast by the moon, there was a kaleidoscope of dazzling lights, shapes, and colors cast by the sun beaming through the leafy branches of the trees. The mature deciduous' were full of birds and squirrels. Cats roamed casually about their colony nestled in this inconspicuous spot within the big city. It was an oasis of nature that momentarily reminded Greta of her childhood, spending long summer days exploring the wilderness at camp in Northern Ontario.

Suddenly, Greta was snapped back to reality by a honking car on Main Street. The bustle of people on the sidewalk told her that she was far from home. She turned left on Main and passed McCluskey's on her way to the coin wash. Once she got to the laundromat, she loaded everything into one washer with a mini box of powdered detergent that she bought from a machine on the wall. While the washer was going, Greta went over to her bank and deposited the cheque from her mother plus most of the money from the books she had returned for refund. She still had a heavy pile of coins in her purse from tips. She'd already used some for the laundry machines.

Exiting the bank she lit a cigarette and smoked it on her way back to the laundromat. While she waited for her clothes in the dryer Greta walked over to the payphone and dialed zero to place a collect call to her mother.

The phone rang several times before her mother picked up, answering it with a lilting, "Hello."

The operator quickly said, "A collect call from Greta. Do you accept the charges?"

"Hi mom," said Greta.

"Oh, is that you Greta?" asked Myra. "Yes, I accept the charges."

"Yes, mom," she replied. "I'm at the laundromat so I thought I'd call you from the payphone here."

"Oh, ok. How are you?" her mother asked.

"I'm fine. But I have something to tell you," said Greta, nervously.

"Did you get the letter I sent you?" asked Myra.

" Yes mom. I got it, thank you," Greta answered.

"Good. How's school going?" asked Myra.

"Well, that's what I want to talk to you about," Greta went on. "I don't like it, so I'm not going to continue."

"Oh. Really?" said Myra in an abrupt manner. "Well, what about the tuition I paid and your apartment?"

"I'm sorry about that mom. Maybe you can get some refund and stop payments," Greta replied.

"Well, isn't that something," Myra huffed.

"I got a job at this place called Joe's Coffee House," Greta responded with a crackle in her throat.

"So you're going to be a waitress?" Myra said derisively.

"Well, yes, for now," answered Greta meekly.

"What kind of job is that?" asked Myra.

"What do you mean? You're a cleaning lady," said Greta.

"Yes. Well. I didn't have the opportunities that you do to make something of yourself," retorted Myra.

"I'm sorry you can't accept me for who I am. That I have to be some-thing, to be some-one. The course just wasn't what I expected it to be," said Greta. "I'd rather be working."

"Well there's nothing I can do about that, is there?" Myra replied matter-of-factly. "Your rent is paid until the end of November. Then you'll have to take care of it yourself."

"I know," said Greta.

"Well I don't know what I'm going to tell everyone and what people are going to think, especially your father," Myra said.

"I don't care what other people think. I just don't want to be in school," said Greta.

"Well it seems you've made up your mind," answered Myra.

"Yes, I have," said Greta.

"Well. Goodbye then," Myra's voice trembled.

"Bye ma," Greta choked.

Each was holding back tears at the end. Greta was so sad for having disappointed her mother and everyone back home who knew she had gone away to college. She would be too embarrassed to ever go back home. The shame was overwhelming. In truth, she was not prepared for the commitment of college or big city life. But there she was alone in the big city, a concrete jungle where she now needed to survive on her own.

With watery eyes, Greta checked on her laundry. It was dry, so she folded everything very carefully to avoid wrinkles as much as possible. She noticed that the pair of pink underwear she wore the day before were not there. She checked the dryer and washing machine to make sure she hadn't missed them. They weren't there either. Maybe she left them on the bathroom floor when she scooped up the pile of dirty clothes. Placing everything carefully back into the garbage bag, Greta took a deep breath and walked briskly back to her apartment.

When she got there, she took the clean clothes out of the bag and placed them in neat piles along the kitchenette counter. She took notice of the unread note from her mother and the unopened envelope from Jeff. Then she looked around the bathroom for her pink underwear and couldn't find them.

"That's so weird," she said out loud to herself.

Shaking her head as if to remove that thought, Greta reset her mind to getting ready for work. She picked up a comb and looked in the mirror parting her hair down the middle from front to back. Then she clipped one side out of the way and wove a French braid down the other side. After a French braid on either side was done she used bobby pins to create an arrangement at the back of her head that looked like coffee bread.

She used the extra time to do Jane Fonda's workout. She hadn't eaten all day and felt in control of her body.

After her workout, she made an instant coffee and began applying foundation to her face.

Taking another look at her uniform, Greta decided to touch it up with the iron, then carefully folded it and placed it in her oversized purse with her only pair of sneakers. They were grey canvas with a white rubber sole.

Checking the time on her clock radio, Greta saw that she had time on her hands so she made an instant cup of soup as a reward for having worked out. She sat at the kitchenette counter and pushed her piles of laundry aside. The unread note from her mother and unopened letter from Jeff taunted her so she reached for the letter from Jeff. She

slid a fingernail under the corner of the seal and tore it open neatly, pulling out the letter and unfolding it. She blew on the hot soup as she read the letter written in a decidedly careful and artful masculine hand.
It read:

Dear Greta, Thank you for the letter you sent. I wasn't expecting it, so it was a pleasant surprise. I know you've only been gone for a few weeks, but it feels like much longer. I hope things are good with you. It must be exciting to be in the big city. I'm working and saving money. I miss hanging out with you, like smoking a few and drinking, and just hanging out or going for walks together. It's not the same here without you. I told you already that Brenda and Mark hooked up and that she's pregnant. They didn't want to get married or anything but they moved in together and are getting ready for the baby. I can't imagine having a baby at our age. I still see them once in a while but it's way different now that they are a couple and starting a family.
Maybe when you get time you can write me again and let me know how you're doing. Or call me sometime if that's easier. It'd be good to hear your voice.
There's a long weekend next month, maybe I can take a day off before and after and come to see you. That's if you want. Anyway, just wanted to let you know that I'm thinking about you. I love the letter you sent. I keep reading it over and over again so I can imagine your voice in my head. I really miss you a lot and I hope I can come to see you soon.
Your friend always.
With Love.
Jeff

Greta felt sad and missed him. He was always there for her back home and he never expected anything in return. They just enjoyed each other's company no matter what they were doing. She put the letter back into the envelope and tucked it in her top dresser drawer along with the unread note from her mother. Her soup had cooled enough to start sipping it while she applied the rest of her makeup over her base foundation.

Soup and makeup finished; she laid on the bed to get her jeans on. Then she put on a camisole, long sleeved cotton blouse, and her flip flops. When she left, she locked the door and tried the handle to make sure it was locked.

Then she traipsed down the alley with her blouse untucked, wafting in the breeze. There was a sense of relief that she had told her mother that she had quit school. The pretty fuchsia camisole Greta wore brightened up the world on that sunny autumn afternoon and her fair skin glowed bronze. Most people looked at her as she passed. Only if they were completely absorbed in a task did they not look. Her beauty was unmistakably wholesome and youthful, and she possessed an effortless sexy confidence. Men and women alike were compelled to take notice of Greta's beauty. Some were jealous and others expressed awe. She arrived fifteen minutes early for work, went to the back room, and changed into her uniform and sneakers.

"I like your hair," said Connie when Greta came onto the dining room floor.

"Thanks. I thought it would be easier like this," answered Greta, in her coffee bread French braids.

"I want you to take the booths today. That will be your section. I'll do the tables and counter," said Connie.

"Sure," Greta said with a smile, "whatever you like."

Greta placed a pad and pen in the front of her apron. She began checking that each booth was clean, set, and stocked with cream, sugar, and the like.

"Greta!" She heard Joe call out loudly from the kitchen.

Greta quickly trotted over to the service window.

"You got two messages. Take five minutes when it's not busy. And use the payphone," he said as he passed her two slips of paper with names and phone numbers on them.

She quickly saw that one was from the laundromat and the other was from Jeans N Tops. She slipped the papers in her apron pocket.

"Thanks Joe," she said with a bright smile.

"No problem," he replied as he went back to cooking and bossing the kitchen staff.

Some customers had sat at a booth so Greta cheerfully got into gear, grabbed four menus and a full pot of fresh coffee.

"Good afternoon. Would you all like coffees?" she asked the foursome.

Three of them said, "Yes please."

But the fourth lady, closest to the window said in a condescending tone, "Tea for me please dear. If it's not too much trouble."

"No trouble at all," replied Greta politely, handing each woman a menu.

They giggled and whispered amongst themselves.

"Don't worry about them," Connie said to Greta when she was getting the tea ready. "They come in every so often and think their shit doesn't stink. But - because they think they're better than us, they'll leave you a big tip."

"No problem," said Greta. "I'll kill 'em with kindness."

Not flustered by the haughtiness of the giggling gaggle, Greta did her job to perfection and they each rewarded her with a big fat tip on separate bills.

Darlene arrived for her shift as Connie was making her last rounds. It was the tail end of the dinner rush and Connie made sure her tables were clean and set for Darlene to take over.

As she brewed some fresh coffee she asked Greta, "Can you check the dessert fridge and restock it with whatever desserts are left in the kitchen freezer please?"

"Will do," replied Greta, looking a little frazzled.

As Darlene came out, she showed Greta the larger tray to take to the freezer to gather the desserts.

"Just wait until your booths aren't too busy though before doing that," said Darlene.

She added, "We get more people at night just wanting dessert and coffee. So we will need it."

"Gotcha. Thanks," Greta replied. "I think I have time now."

Things were hectic that night but Greta kept up, and her feet were much better with the sneakers although she felt short. She was leaning into a booth as she was wiping it down when she saw Cory and Graham walking past. They didn't notice her in the window. She had not been to McCluskey's since the night she met Daryl. She put four paper placemats down as the bells on the restaurant door chimed. As she was placing cutlery she glanced toward the door. It was them. Cory nudged Graham as he pointed at Greta. They said something inaudible and walked towards her. Greta smiled softly at the handsome young men.

"Wow! I didn't know you worked here," said Cory.

He smiled widely as the two slid into the booth that Greta had just finished setting. She removed two of the place settings and centered the other two in front of them.

"Yes. Nice to see you guys. Can I bring you some coffee?" she asked, trying not to smile too broadly because it made her cheeks look chubby.

"You bet," they exclaimed. "It's really cool to see you."

"Great to see you too," she replied.

They watched her walk away. When she looked back, they averted their eyes. She returned and filled their coffee cups, leaving enough room for cream.

"We don't actually need menus hon," said Cory.

"Yeah, we know what we want," said Graham.

"What'll it be then?" asked Greta, pulling out her pad and pen.

Cory ordered a pastrami on rye and Graham a BLT. She kept their coffee cups full as she circulated between customers. And when there was a lull in activity she used the payphone to call the laundromat and Jeans N Tops. They both requested an in-person interview with her for the following day; the laundromat at 10 am and Jeans N Tops at 1 pm. Greta was excited at the prospect of getting a second job because she needed to plan for paying her own rent very soon.

Cory and Graham lingered over their coffees and chatted with Greta at every chance they got.

"We haven't seen you at McCluskey's since the night we met," said Cory.

"We're going to shoot some pool there tonight," Graham chimed in. "Why don't you come and meet us there when you get off?"

" Sounds like fun," Greta replied as she removed their empty plates. "Dessert for either of you? The apple pie is to die for."

"My favourite," said Cory. "I'll have a piece."

"Cherry a la mode if you have it," said Graham.

"I sure do. Coming right up," answered Greta.

"You can make mine a la mode too," said Graham.

They ate every morsel of their desserts and left Greta a healthy tip with some final words of encouragement to join them at the bar later.

Greta's apron was becoming noticeably weighted with tip money. Darlene said, "You know, I can change your tips into bills if you want. We always need change for the cash register."

"Seriously?" Greta replied. "That would be great."

She dumped her apron out on the lower ledge of the counter and began counting out the quarters, then the dimes, and so forth. It reminded her of counting her dad's poker winnings. She was surprised at how plenteous her tips were, and there was still another hour until closing time. Greta jumped at the opportunity to serve more customers as the chimes rang and a group of cheerful young adults came in the door and sat at an empty booth. They still had time to order food from the kitchen so she brought menus and a coffee pot.

She was energized by the busy shift and the generous tips. At ten o'clock, Joe came out of the kitchen, removed the tray from the till and sat in the last booth. Greta made a point to ask him if she could get him anything. He politely asked for coffee with cream and told her to get something to eat and join him. Even though she wasn't really hungry, she'd only had instant soup that day. So she got a carrot muffin and a coffee and sat with Joe while Darlene cleaned up the back counter.

"Everything ok today?" he asked.

"Yes. Great. Thank you," Greta replied as she moistened the bite of muffin in her mouth with a sip of coffee.

"You can do same shifts next week?" Joe asked.

"Yes. Definitely," answered Greta.

"Ok," said Joe without lifting his eyes from the money he continued counting.

Greta stood up after finishing her muffin and put the dirty dishes in the tray near the kitchen door. She took a damp cloth and the coffee pot over to Joe. She refreshed his coffee and wiped down the spot where she had been.

"Good night," she said.

Joe responded with an indecipherable, part word, part grunt, as he continued counting without lifting his eyes.

Greta checked in with Darlene to see if there were any other tasks she wanted her to do before passing the broom through the restaurant.

"No. You go ahead and sweep," she told her.

Later in the back room, Greta changed from her uniform into her tight jeans, fuchsia camisole, and blouse. Darlene was changing her shoes and left her work shoes there because she worked full-time.

"You seem to be getting the hang of things pretty fast," said Darlene.

"Oh thanks. I like it. But my feet took a shit kicking yesterday," Greta laughed.

"Yeah, I could see that. You won't make that mistake again," snorted Darlene.

Greta removed her French braids and ran her fingers through her hair to loosen up the waves they created. She took a couple of bobby pins and pulled a few strands off of her face, leaving a sultry fringe. Quickly touching up her powder and lipstick, Greta then hurriedly caught up to Darlene who was already heading for the door.

"I'm coming!" she called after her.

"Come on girl. I wanna go home," said Darlene in a firm voice.

Joe was done counting and was back in the kitchen bossing the staff around back there. Darlene and Greta exited by the front door and Darlene locked up as usual.

They said good night as they started in different directions.

"See you next week," Greta said cheerfully.

Then she lit a cigarette on her way to drop her uniform off at her apartment before continuing to McCluskey's. She hid her nervousness when she arrived, worried that Daryl might be there.

The old man was a fixture at the end of the bar. He made eye contact with Greta who quickly averted her eyes and scanned the room. There was a layer of cigarette smoke that hovered like smog above her eye level and the familiar odor of beer stained carpet permeated the stagnant air. Years of drunken foot traffic had worn faded trails throughout the room as if to welcome any soul who needed a drink to follow the path. Greta walked straight to the bar and stood on her tiptoes because she had forgotten to change out of her flip flops, emphasizing her petite stature. The familiar bartender offered reassurance that she would not to be asked for identification.

She swept back her voluminous unbraided hair. The sun-kissed crimps cascaded around her, reflecting the dim amber light. Her hair was her crowning glory that night.

"What can I get for you dear?" asked the amenable bartender.

"I'll have a draft please," replied Greta, opting for cheap beer instead of an expensive cocktail.

The old man at the end of the bar stared at Greta with a toothy grin as she waited for her glass of draft.

"There you are, darling," said the bartender as he placed the glass of beer in front of Greta.

She passed him a bill and waited for the change. Having learned some of the etiquette of tipping after two days of waitressing at Joe's, she gave him a modest tip. The bartender slid it off the bar with a smile and a wink of acknowledgement.

Greta took the glass of beer in her hand and pirouetted towards the pool tables. Catching a glimpse through the crowd, sure enough the young men who patronized Joe's earlier that evening were in the midst of a match. With many eyes checking her out, Greta strutted towards them.

Cory and Graham stood up straighter when she approached and placed the butts of their pool cues on the floor.

"Hey. You made it," said Cory with a big bright smile.

" Have a seat," added Graham.

"Right here," he said as he rushed to pull out a chair for her. Greta breathed a sigh of relief to finally be able to sit down. Her feet were tired. Graham refilled her glass from the pitcher of draft on the table. And when Greta pulled out a cigarette Cory quickly took a lighter out of his pocket and lit it for her. Every time her glass was almost empty one of the men refilled it. They ordered another pitcher when the waitress came back around.

"Wait!" Cory said to the waitress.

" Do you like tequila?" he asked Greta.

"Yeah, who doesn't?" she replied, never having had it before.

"A round of snake bites!" Graham shouted.

"You got it," replied the waitress.

She returned with three shot glasses of clear fluid, a saltshaker and a small dish with three wedges of lime. Greta had no idea what to do so she imitated Cory and Graham. First, she licked the pudgy part of her left hand below the meeting of the thumb and index finger. She shook a generous amount of salt onto the wet spot. She placed a piece of lime in the same hand, making sure not to spill the salt. She raised the shot glass in her right hand and watched Cory and Graham lick the salt off of their hands, drink their entire shots and bite into their lime wedges. Greta followed suit without hesitation so as not to show her lack of experience and they all squinted as their shot glasses smacked the table rhythmically. It was like winning a challenge. The powerful potion burned going down and then rose with a warm buzz in her head. They all laughed boisterously and continued drinking draft and smoking cigarettes.

"You wanna play a game Greta?" asked Cory.

"I don't know how," said Greta.

"I'll teach ya," he said.

"Well I'll give it a shot," she giggled.

Cory showed Greta how to choose a pool cue by rolling it across the surface of the pool table to see if it was wobbly or straight. Since Greta was petite, he suggested a cue that wasn't too long or too cumbersome for learning. They agreed on one together and Cory racked the balls and broke them with one powerful stroke of the cue stick. Greta couldn't help but feel a little impressed as she watched the balls roll in every direction, two of them dropping into corner pockets. Cory explained that he could choose either stripe or solid because one of each had gone down. He called his shot and missed on the solid.

"Now you can shoot any ball because I missed," he said.

Greta awkwardly grasped the pool cue and pointed it at the cue ball in line with a striped ball near a corner pocket. Cory offered her instruction on how to hold the cue stick and how to make a bridge. She placed her whole left hand on the pool table with her fingers spread out like a spider. Then she arched her knuckles and lifted her thumb resting the cue stick in the crevice by her thumb. As she leaned over the pool table and took aim Cory stretched his long lean and toned arms over hers.

"Like this," he said as he helped her with her position.

His groin rubbed up against her buttocks, causing him an erection. Greta took the shot and the stripe went down. She jumped up and down, looking at Cory in delight as he calmed his hormones.

"Nicely done," he said.

"You can shoot again," he said as he took two steps towards their table to grab his glass of draft beer.

"You're stripe and I'm solid," he declared.

"Ok. Let's see now," said Greta.

She slowly walked around the table trying to assess which striped ball to try next. After consulting with Cory, she stretched her body over the table again, skintight jeans hugging her curves. The fuchsia camisole she wore clung to her half-exposed cleavage exposing her breasts when she leaned over. Cory was aroused by Greta's crimped blonde tresses draped over the pool table. Her unabashed sex appeal attracted many onlookers. They finished the game with Cory cleaning up but giving Greta lots of chances to learn as he watched her every scintillating move. Then they rejoined Graham who had ordered a basket of chicken wings that had just arrived.

"Dig in guys," he said as they sat down simultaneously. "There's another pitcher coming."

Greta wasn't hungry but slowly nibbled on a couple of wings while the young men devoured what was in the basket.

"Last call," said the waitress as she took away the basket of bones.

"Bring us another round of shooters," said Cory.

Graham asked the waitress for another basket of wings and another pitcher of draft. They would have an hour until closing time to finish it all. She brought the pitcher, shots, and lime first. The salt was already on the table. Knowing what to do now, Greta salted her hand, downed the shot in one quick gulp, and bit into the lime wedge. The lime juices tamed the burn of the fiery liquid. Their shot glasses hit the table in a rhythmic slam, slam, slam. They laughed, smoked cigarettes and drank more draft until the waitress brought the basket of wings. Graham and Cory both pulled out their wallets to pay the cheque.

Graham said, "I got it! It's my turn."

Cory replied, "Glad you're keeping track."

Greta was getting thoroughly soused as the men inhaled the wings and draft. When they left, they hung around outside for a while talking. Each lit a cigarette. Then Greta realized that Cory was passing her a joint. She took it and inhaled deeply, coughing on the exhale.

"The West End Cafe is open 24 hours if you guys wanna grab a coffee," said Cory.

All in agreement, they finished the joint and started walking. They passed the laundromat that Greta used. In her wobbly condition, she grabbed Cory's arm for support. Cory and Graham were like Goliaths flanking Greta who was determined to keep up with them. By the time they reached The West End Cafe, Greta was hanging onto Cory's waist. In her stupor, she was relieved to be seated.

As quickly as she'd sat down, she got back up.

"I'll have a coffee. But I gotta go to the bathroom first," she told the guys.

Greta saw the public washroom sign and staggered in that direction. She pushed the door, entered a stall and immediately began to hurl. Pulling her hair back with one hand Greta saw the bits of undigested chicken and brown foam from the muffin she had eaten at Joe's. She flushed, peed, and flushed again. Her mouth tasted like puke and burning tequila. She rinsed her mouth with water and shoved a stick of gum in her mouth, chewing it aggressively to release the flavor. Her eyes were red and watery. She powdered her face, fluffed her hair, and put on more lipstick before spitting out the gum. She took a deep breath and returned to the table.

Graham and Cory were talking about work. She sat down beside Cory and quietly put sweetener and a generous amount of cream in her coffee. She feared drinking it black would upset her stomach. Cory slipped his hand under the table and put it on Greta's knee. Greta let it rest there without objection and sipped on her sweet creamy coffee in silence.

Cory offered her a cigarette.

"You ok?" he asked.

"Yeah, fine," she replied, drawing on the cigarette as Cory lit it for her.

The young men continued talking about work without any bother about Greta's silence. Whenever she reached the bottom of her coffee the waitress efficiently refilled it.

"Are you ready to order?" she asked.

Greta quickly said, "Nothing for me, thanks."

"Can we get a large fry Nancy?" Cory asked, seeming to be on familiar terms with her.

"Anything for you hon," the waitress flirtatiously replied.

Graham and Cory shared the large basket of fries.

They chatted up the waitress each time she came to check on them. She was middle-aged and showed a lot of her soft cleavage.

"We have a divine devil's food cake. It's super moist," Nancy enticed Cory and Graham to stay longer.

"I could handle that," said Graham.

Greta almost passed out a couple of times. And when the men had eaten and drank their fill, and exhausted their conversation, Cory asked for the cheque.

He gave Nancy some bills and said, ``keep the change sweetie."

Outside, Graham said, "I'll see you tomorrow."

And he walked away.

Then Cory looked at Greta and said, "I'll walk you home."

Her eyes had cleared up and her roughness was muted by the dim evening light. They headed back in the direction from where they'd come.

"Where abouts do you live?" asked Cory.

"Just past McCluskey's," replied Greta, holding onto Cory's arm for stability.

"Not far," she slurred.

"Okay, no problem. It's a nice night for a walk," he said.

There was a clear sky but even though the full moon was visible, the streetlights overpowered most of the stars.

When they passed McCluskey's, Greta said, "It's this way."

They had reached the entrance to the alley, which she now called the catwalk.

"There are a bunch of cats that live down here," she said.

The catwalk was filled with long swaying shadows created by the moon, city lights, and the night breeze dancing with the trees. Greta faltered when she heard the bang and screech of two cats quarrelling near the abandoned garbage bin. The clowder was especially active that night.

Cory reassured her by saying, "It's just two cats mating."

"Really?" said Greta.

"Yeah. They make a lot of noise when they mate," he said.

"Oh? Ok," said Greta, in Cory's firm embrace.

"Nothing to worry about," continued Cory.

The moon reflected in his deep brown eyes and his shaggy brown hair fluttered in the evening breeze. His body was firm and muscular from working as a furniture mover. She felt safe with Cory in that moment. The catwalk that was usually creepy and intimidating at night, suddenly felt like a private hollow where Greta could do anything with Cory.

He pulled out a joint and lit it. After heightening her buzz, Greta lucidly got caught up in the visual sensations of the shadows of the swaying branches. They slowly walked the catwalk, her arm around his waist, and his arm around her shoulder. They emerged beneath the streetlight where the alley met the sidewalk nearly across from Greta's apartment.

She pointed, "I'm just over there."

They lingered under the streetlight for a while, staring into each other's eyes. Even in her state of intoxication, Greta was a raving beauty with bloodshot blue eyes. She felt he was looking at the depths of her soul. In that moment, he was a stallion of irresistible masculinity.

With no words, they walked slowly across the street together, down the driveway and down the stairway to Greta's apartment door. She rummaged around her purse, pulled out her key, and unlocked the door.

They entered the apartment; Cory closed the door behind them. He embraced her and gave her a long wet passionate kiss. Without resistance she kissed him in return as their mouths opened on each other and their tongues swirled. Cory slowly moved Greta backwards, towards the bed, and laid her down while continuing to kiss her with open mouth and undulating tongue. Greta did not resist when Cory put a cupped hand on her breast.

"Are you on the pill?" he asked in between kisses.

"No," answered Greta, stopping.

Cory stopped and grunted.

"But you are so hot and I want you," he said.

"I want you too," said Greta pleadingly.

He started kissing her again, softly, on the lips. He swept her hair back and looked into her watery blue eyes as he began massaging her breast. Without resistance, she softly moaned. He unzipped and pulled down her jeans as she wiggled her hips cooperatively. Then he slid his hand down the front of her panties and cupped her hot hairy pubis.

"Lay back," Cory whispered.

And she did.

He slid her jeans off the rest of the way and dropped them on the floor. Next, he removed her panties as she thought about the erotic magazines from back home. She spread herself as he inserted a finger.

"Oh, you're so warm and wet," said Cory looking at her with pure lust.

He uncovered her breast and suckled as she arched. She hummed as he stimulated her insides and breasts simultaneously. He slid her petite frame up to the pillows and pushed her legs apart. He lowered his head into her crotch and penetrated her with his long, thick tongue. He swirled and licked his way up to her engorged nub as a sudden rush of uninhibited adrenaline roused Greta to her knees. Taking control, she guided Cory onto his back and put her mouth around his throbbing member. It vibrated, swelled, and stiffened as she stayed there for a while, sucking and tasting his saltiness. Then she straddled Cory while grasping his erection and slid herself over the oozing tip.

"Oh my God," said Cory, eyes wide open, staring at Greta's thin body, concave stomach, and engorged breasts with erect nipples.

He squeezed her breasts, feeling their fullness and wet his fingers with saliva to lubricate her nipples. His manhood penetrated her fully as she became profusely wet and began to writhe. With the optimal lubrication Greta rode Cory like he was a wild stallion beneath her loins. The deep penetration and friction caused Greta to cry out.

"Oh! Oh!" she wailed.

Cory held her hip bones as she bounced up and down. She gyrated forward and back, so that her clitoris rubbed on his pubic bone while his phallus pushed on her cervix.

Again she cried out, "Oh, Oh, Oh!"

There was a culmination of erotic ecstasy. She released a long drawn out sigh as quivers radiated from her genitals, across her abdomen, and throughout her entire body in rushing waves of adrenaline. Cory flipped her over and pushed her flexible legs over her head pumping his phallus into her until his semen was deposited in a final thrilling ejaculation of thick cum.

They laid beside each other, slippery with sweat. They breathed hot and heavy, as if they had just run a marathon. Greta draped her arm across his chest and her leg across his thigh and passed out. It was her first time.

Chapter 9
Lost Identity

She squinted as the sun hit her eyes through a crack in the curtains. Alone again, her hazy head wasn't sure what may or may not have happened the night before.

She went to the bathroom and the burn of her pee confirmed her experience with Cory.

Her aches were soothed by the hot spray of the shower as she lathered away the lingering carnal sweat from the night before. Still nauseous and dizzy, she suddenly remembered that she had two job interviews to go to.

She turned off the shower and grabbed the towel off the toilet seat. She patted herself dry and wrapped the towel around her head. It was 9:30. She missed her first interview.

So she drank two tall glasses of water, set her alarm, put on her comfy sweats and crawled back into bed. With the towel wrapped around her head she fell back to sleep in the smell of Cory's pheromones.

After an hour, the buzzer blared. She woke from a dreamless sleep into chaotic broken memories. She knew she had unprotected sex with Cory.

She needed to get ready for her job interview. She removed the towel from her head releasing her damp scrunched tresses. While her hair air-dried, she applied a light moisturizer to her face and drank more water. She made an instant coffee hoping it would take the edge off. She was still woozy and her thoughts were fragmented. She reset her alarm so she would get a warning when it was time to leave. Then she continued with her makeup. Bronze shadow on her eyelids contrasted with her tired crystal blue eyes. Dark brown mascara was soft over her delicate translucent lashes. A light sweep of baby pink blush on the apples of her cheeks and frosty pink lip gloss added a touch of sparkle. Her hair and face needed to land her a job in the jeans store. She just had to get there.

So she put on her best pair of jeans and the only pair of black pumps she had with a knee high stocking. She wore a red lace camisole topped with a lovely handmade black blouse and left a few buttons open to allow the lace to peek out. Her teardrop red coral earrings were the only accessory.

It wasn't until Greta was leaving that she realized the apartment door had been unlocked since Cory left her in the middle of the night. She tried to push Cory out of her mind. She turned off her alarm before it went off and left.

As she started up the catwalk she lit a cigarette and walked briskly towards Main Street. Her freshly washed hair had only been combed lightly with her fingers. Having slept with the towel on her head accentuated it's natural waves. Her hair bounced with each step and she felt confident in her body. Many heads turned to watch Greta pass, but she paid no heed as her mind was intermittently flashing back to her foray into intercourse.

She needed to land that second job to be able to afford rent. So she forged ahead thinking about work. Before she knew it, she had reached Young Street and could see the sign for Jeans N Tops. Feeling a little nervous but emboldened by her first sexual escapade, Greta crossed the intersection with the mass of metropolitan people. She maintained a calm pace as she approached the store and opened the door. She walked up to the cashier's counter.

"Hello, I'm Greta. I have an interview for the sales position," she said.

"Oh. Ok. I'll get the manager," answered a spritely young woman with dark straight hair and brown complexion.

Greta looked around the store which was full of trendy clothes. A middle-aged man with some grey in his beard and a turban on his head walked towards her.

"Hello, I'm Harbinder," he said with a strong accent. "You can come with me."

"Pleased to meet you," she said.

She followed him to the back of the store and into his office.

"Please sit down," said Harbinder with a big smile.

Taking a seat in the cramped office, Greta sat up straight and smiled confidently.

"I'm looking for someone on our busy days for sales," said Harbinder. "Thursday and Friday afternoons until closing time and all day Saturday."

"Oh, that's great," said Greta, "I'm available and honestly that works perfectly with my schedule."

"You ever do sales before?" asked Harbinder. "I don't see it on your application."

"Not yet," Greta replied. "But I am very good with people and I'm a very quick learner."

"I can give you a try," he said, looking her up and down. "We see if it works out."

"Yes, that would be fine," said Greta.

"I can't wait to start," she added, in an effort to show her enthusiasm.

"I will get Jenna to show you around right now. And you start tomorrow," said Harbinder.

"Thank you very much," said Greta as she restrained her excitement in favor of a more mature demeanor.

"Come. I introduce you," said Harbinder as he walked ahead of her to the store front.

"Jenna, this is Greta. She starts tomorrow afternoon. Can you show her around the store a little bit please?" he asked.

"Sure. Hi Greta," said Jenna. "Come on, I'll show you around. You'll get to know where everything is very quickly I'm sure."

"Thanks," Greta replied.

She followed Jenna with the long dark hair and brown complexion.

After her introduction and orientation, Greta jaunted back to her apartment at a brisk pace. As soon as she entered, she kicked off her pumps, stripped and put her comfy sweats back on. She removed the sex and sweat stained sheets from her bed and stuffed them into a garbage bag with the rest of her dirty clothes. She took a bunch of coins from the jar under the sink for laundry.
Slinging the hefty bag over her shoulder, Greta briskly walked to the laundromat in her flip flops. She stuffed the bedding into one machine. Her jeans and everything else went to another.

She went to the payphone and dialed zero.

"Operator, how may I help you?" said a woman on the line.

"I'd like to make a long-distance call and charge it to my home phone please," said Greta.

"I'll need the number you want me to charge it to and the number you want to call," said the operator.

After providing the numbers she heard the line ringing.

He answered, "Hello."

"It's me, Greta," she said.

"Oh hi! I'm glad you called. How's it going? Did you get my letter? How do you like college?" he asked.

"Slow down," Greta replied. "Yes. I got your letter. It was very sweet and I miss you so much."

"Yeah. Well, things just aren't the same around here without you," said Jeff. "Can you believe Brenda is having a baby? Like wow."

"Yeah. You told me. She'll probably be a good mom," Greta replied. "Especially since she's got Mark by her side."

"Yeah. He's gonna be a good dad too," said Jeff. "He seems pretty stoked about it. But what about you? How ya doing?"

"I'm good," said Greta. "But things aren't going quite as originally planned."

"What do you mean?" he asked.

"I hated the whole school routine and all the books and the class schedule and the atmosphere there," she paused. "Everyone was so snobby and in their own bubble. So I quit."

"Really?" responded Jeff. "What'd your parents say?"

"My ma was like the usual. All she cared about was what everyone else would think," said Greta. "But there's nothing she can do, so she's pissed. Whatever, I'd rather work."

"Oh yeah. I get that," said Jeff. "I'm working lots lately and I love making the dough."

"Yeah. Me too," said Greta, pretending she wasn't worried about making ends meet.

"I'm working at Joe's Coffee House two days a week and just got hired at Jeans N Tops three shifts. I'm so excited. It's gonna be way cool."

They continued trying to convince each other that their choices were right and that they were happy with their lives. Jeff repeated how much he missed Greta and that he wanted to see her so badly. Greta humored Jeff saying, "Well, you could always come down for a visit if you want."

"Oh yeah," answered Jeff. "I'm gonna plan a long weekend to come down. For sure."

Neither of them was very confident that would happen but they dreamed about it for the moment.

"I've gotta go," said Greta. "My laundry is ready to go into the dryer."

"Okay," answered Jeff. "Write me back when you get the time."

"Ok. I will," said Greta.

"I miss you," said Jeff.

"I know. I miss you too," Greta replied.

As she hung up the phone a lump formed in her throat. She didn't realize until then how much she missed Jeff and how he cared about her unconditionally.

She put her laundry in two dryers and sat down with a cigarette. She looked through some cheap tabloids then chatted with an older lady who was folding warm clothes.

After the woman left, Greta carefully folded her laundry to reduce wrinkling. She was in no hurry to get back to an empty apartment. But it was getting dark and she hated walking the catwalk at night. Now it was unavoidable.

It was overcast and the catwalk was pitch black. The trees seemed to block even the city lights that night. There were the sounds of muffled traffic, cats rummaging through the garbage, and the slapping of her flip flops on the bottom of her feet. The streetlight at the end of the catwalk guided her to the relative safety of visibility.

As she approached her apartment, she could see through a slit between the curtains that a light was on. She was sure she had turned them all out. With her key prepared, she saw the door was open a crack. She entered and saw Charlie looking through her dresser drawer.

"What are you doing?!" she yelled.

Surprised by her discovery, he stood up straight and stuttered, "Um, I need to inspect all the electrical outlets in the units because there was a blown breaker earlier today."

"Are there outlets inside my dresser?" she asked him. "I don't think you should be in here without notifying me ahead of time."

Charlie walked across the room towards Greta and said, "I wasn't able to contact you. I'm sorry for the inconvenience."

"If there's nothing else. I'd like you to leave please," said Greta.

He got behind her and kicked the apartment door. It shut with a slam.

"I'll make sure to let you know the next time I am coming," he said.

"I should hope so," said Greta. "Now I think you should leave."

"I still have an inspection to finish," Charlie replied.

With a change of tone he moved closer to her. She backed away. She still had the key in her hand.

"I don't think so," said Greta. "Please leave."

She was scared but strong.

"I see how you dress when you leave this place," said Charlie.

"What do you mean?" Greta questioned.

"With your tight jeans and all that makeup," Charlie continued. "You're nothing but a horny little slut."

"What?" she asked. "I was just going to work."

"Oh… working now, eh. I have a job for you," he said as he grabbed her hair and forced his mouth on hers.

She squirmed free.

"Stop it!" she yelled as she gouged his neck with her key.

"You bitch!" he yelled.

He punched her in the face.

"Help! Help!" she screamed.

"Shut up! You little slut," he said as he lunged toward her and placed his hand over her mouth.

"Don't you say another word, bitch!" he demanded.

Greta was so scared she wanted to cry.

He slapped her hard across the face causing her lip to bleed and the key to fall out of her hand. She fell to her knees and began to cry.

"I said shut up," he commanded as he pulled Greta's missing panties from his pocket.

They smelled like chemicals. He pulled her up by her hair as he balled up the panties and shoved them in her mouth. Then he turned her around, pushed her over the end of the undressed bed and pulled her sweatpants down while holding her hair tight. Greta was bleeding from her lip and her scalp hurt while she struggled, mumbled, and choked.

He pushed her face down onto the bed and told her to be quiet or she'd regret it as he shoved his penis into her from behind. Greta was still raw from her first time having sex the night before. It burned so bad and she cried harder. He pushed into her with his full force until he ejaculated. Pulling himself out, he zipped his pants and left the apartment, leaving her without another word.

Greta lay there on the undressed bed crying for most of the night before getting up and going to the bathroom to sit on the toilet. It burned when she peed and when she patted her raw genitals with toilet paper there was bright red blood. She wasn't sure if it was from what Charlie did, or if she had started her period. She had forgotten when her last period was and the blood was brighter than her usual menstrual flow. She examined her genitalia with a handheld mirror. They were raw and red but she couldn't see where the blood was coming from.

Distraught, she looked in the mirror and was horrified at her red swollen eyes, the cut on her swollen lip and the smeared dried blood across her face. Her hair was a complete mess and she cried again at her reflection. She was starting her new job at the jeans store that afternoon and couldn't afford to not make it. Taking a deep breath, Greta turned the shower on to a tepid temperature and stepped in. She poured a generous amount of shampoo into her palm and smoothed it carefully over her head as clumps of hair came out in her hands. She piled the hair in the corner of the tub so it wouldn't clog the drain. The suds from her hair rinsed down the rest of her body. Her painful genitals were soothed by the tepid water. She made it cooler to numb herself and stood there as time stood paused.

She shivered, snapped back to reality, and turned off the water. Slowly she stepped out onto the cold bare floor. She soaked a facecloth with cold water, squeezing out the excess. She laid down with the cold cloth on her face. Once the coolness had faded away, she got up and made her bed with clean bedding. It couldn't mask what had happened there over the past two nights. She had lost her virginity. Now, her identity was lost.

Taking a deep breath, Greta applied moisturizer to her face and dabbed Vaseline on her cut lip. The swelling had gone down and she was determined to hide it. She also ran different scenarios through her mind of likely stories of how she may have cut her lip by accident, like slipping while getting out of the tub and hitting her face on the corner of the vanity. Maybe she forgot to close the cupboard door before going to bed and walked into it when going for a drink of water in the middle of the night.

She plugged in her curling iron and moussed up her hair, being careful not to get any on the sensitive spot on her scalp. Then she gently blow dried her hair upside down. Once it was dry, she looked at the back with a handheld mirror and the vanity mirror. There was a definite bald spot that was very red and raw.

She got a pair of kitchen scissors. Then she lifted all of her hair straight up in her fist and cut it six inches about her head. Letting it fall, she gently combed it out and began to curl it, using hairspray on each piece. The hairspray stung where her hair had been pulled out. She simply lopped off any uneven lengths to the shoulder. Curled and backcombed, she arranged it to cover the bald spot. Checking over and over in the mirrors, she managed to conceal her scalp wound and finished with a coat of Final Net.

Taking a deep breath, Greta lined her lips red and filled them with dark red lipstick. Rather than trying to conceal the fat lip, she decided to work with and emphasize a plump pucker. She put on a subdued brown eyeshadow, bronzer, and dark brown mascara. Satisfied with the transformation, she could go to work and use one of her cover stories if anyone remarked on her lip.
Greta forcefully embraced her new image. She formed an unplanned resilience, deciding that no one had to know what happened if she didn't talk about it.

When she got back to her apartment after her first shift at Jeans N Tops, she removed her makeup and gently brushed the tacky spray out of her hair with the help of some baby powder. Then she opened the drawer where she had tucked away the note from her mother, reminded by the vision of Charlie rummaging through her drawers.

It was written before Greta told her she quit school. It was so brief, and read:

Dear Greta, I hope your course is getting off to a good start and that you are studying. Spend your money wisely and call or write to me when you get a chance. You probably don't have much free time, but you should find a church and see if you can use their piano to keep up with that. I'm sure you're busy and I wish you good luck. Love, Mom

She always wished there was more substance between her and her mother and felt depressed because of everything lacking in herself and their relationship. It was always about what she was doing and if she was accomplishing something meritorious. Greta's feelings, thoughts, likes and dislikes were not part of the equation.

All she ever felt was that she was a disappointment to her and that her life should be planned, not lived. It made her miss Jeff more. Then she dragged the loveseat in front of the apartment door and cried herself to sleep with the kitchen scissors in her hand.

Chapter 10
Perfume and Jazz

Greta got used to her new style and actually felt like it made her look more mature. The season was changing to autumn and she began to wear darker colors, especially black with chunky costume jewelry. She continued to wear dark red on her lips and switched to black mascara and eyeliner. The soft sultry sun-kissed look of Greta's once flowing tresses, and the subtle pinks and browns were gone. Greta no longer feared walking down the catwalk alone at night. She held the scissors in her hand.

Her period still hadn't started three weeks later and all she could do was keep waiting. She looked through the phone book at the laundromat to find doctors and clinics in the area. One morning when she was doing her laundry, she called an office nearby and asked if she could get an appointment. They asked her a few questions and she told the receptionist that she was late for her period.

"So you need a pregnancy test?" asked the receptionist.

"Yes," answered Greta.

"When was your last pap?" asked the receptionist.

"I've never had one," answered Greta.

"Ok. We'll book you in for a full physical and a pap since you're new to us," said the receptionist. "Can you come on Friday at 11 am?"

"Yes, that works for me," said Greta.

"Make sure to bring your health card," said the receptionist.

"Yes. I will," replied Greta.

She didn't even know what a pap was, but she knew she needed to see a doctor in case she was pregnant.

When she arrived for her appointment that Friday morning, a nurse asked her into an examination room where she was asked to undress and put on a hospital gown.

"I see from the notes here that this is your first pap," said the nurse.

"Yes," said Greta.

"You are quite thin," said the nurse.

"When was your last period?" she asked.

"I'm not exactly sure," said Greta, "about six weeks ago I think."

"Is it normal for you to be that late or to miss periods?" asked the nurse.

"No," answered Greta.

"Are you on birth control?" asked the nurse.

"No," answered Greta.

"Are you sexually active?" asked the nurse.

"Yes," said Greta.

"Do you use another form of protection?" asked the nurse.

"No," answered Greta.

"When was the last time you had intercourse?" asked the nurse.

"A little over three weeks ago," said Greta.

"Ok," said the nurse. "I'm going to get you to take this cup to the washroom right there and give me a urine sample please."

Once Greta did that, the nurse took the sample and told her to have a seat on the examination table and the doctor would be with her shortly.

A male doctor entered the exam room wearing a white lab coat with many pockets. A stethoscope hung around his neck, and his nametag read Dr. R. Pigeon. He had the clip board the nurse had been writing on in his hand. After a quick glance at the papers he looked at Greta and used his hands to feel the glands around her neck. He listened to her chest with the cold stethoscope pressed between her breasts.

"You smoke?" asked the doctor.

"Yes," Greta answered.

"You should quit," said the doctor. "It's not good for you. And it might help you put on some weight too."

Then he called for the nurse to come into the room and told Greta to lay down and put her feet into the cold steel stirrups at the end of the table.

"Bring your bottom closer to the end of the table," said the doctor.

Greta tensed up and did what the doctor said.

"Don't worry, just relax," said the nurse. "It's easier if you relax."

Greta took a deep breath as the doctor inserted his gloved and lubricated fingers into her vagina and did a pelvic examination. The nurse handed the doctor a steel instrument that he inserted deeply into her. She flinched.

He said, "Stay still please."

The nurse held Greta's hand as she looked away towards the wall.

"Now I'm going to take a scraping with a little brush," said the doctor.

"It might bleed a little. But that's normal," he added.

"It's almost over," said the nurse. "Breathe and relax."

Greta took a deep breath and it was done. The doctor jammed a few large tissues into the crack of Greta's crotch.

"You can lie back now," he said.

"Any lumps or swelling of your breasts," asked the doctor.

"No," said Greta.

"I should check anyway," he said. "Pull your gown down please."

The nurse left the room with the used instruments and the brush that was used to scrape her cervical cells.

The doctor spent an uncomfortable amount of time examining Greta's breasts as he felt their texture and density. At one point, she thought he was getting pleasure out of the procedure and taking too long.

"They feel fine. Maybe a little bit dense. But nothing to worry about," he commented.

"We will call you with the test results," he added.

"I don't have a phone yet. Can you call me at work please?" asked Greta.

"Yes. Just give the receptionist the number before you leave," said the doctor.

"If everything is negative. Do you want to start the pill?" he asked.

"Yes. I would," she answered.

"Ok, we'll set you up with that after the test results come back," he said as he opened the door.

"And try to eat more. You're too thin," he added and disappeared.

Feeling violated, Greta got dressed after using the bathroom where she wiped the blood and lubricant from her crotch.

Leaving both of her work phone numbers with the receptionist, Greta found a public washroom to freshen up. She lit a cigarette and headed for Jeans N Tops.

Greta was earning commissions on her sales and was familiar with the operations of the store now. Harbinder asked Greta to start training in the office on bookkeeping. She liked being on the floor dealing with customers but also liked the opportunity to be off her feet and doing something new. There was a two-way mirror in the office so Harbinder could watch what was happening on the sales floor. It was Friday night, about an hour before closing, and it was a frosty fall evening.

A scantily clad woman with bare legs, no jacket or sweater, and high heeled sandals came into the store. She had bleached blonde hair with about two inches of dark roots. She clutched a big black purse as she shivered and pretended to be shopping. But her blotchy white skin clearly showed she was freezing. They watched her from the office through the two-way mirror. Greta watched Harbinder take a large wad of bills from his pocket and remove a five dollar bill.

"Go give this to that woman and tell her to use it for bus fare," he said.

Greta took the money and discretely offered it to the woman, telling her that the boss said it was for the bus. It was more than enough to catch the bus and go to a coffee shop so the woman took it and left without a word.

When she went back to the office Harbinder was closing up the books for the day and told Greta to spend the rest of her shift on the sales floor with Jenna.

There was no sign that Greta had ever had a cut on her lip anymore. It had healed quickly and no one made mention of it even if they had noticed. Everyone said they liked her new hairstyle and Greta went on with life as usual, carrying the weight of the worry that she might be pregnant to herself.

She didn't have time that night to think about anything but getting ready for the next day and resting. Her makeup techniques were effective at hiding the strange colors of the healing bruises. They had gone from purple, to green and yellow.

On Saturday, Harbinder wanted Greta on the sales floor helping customers, not in the office. There was a new style of jeans that had come in and Harbinder asked Greta to try them on to see how they looked. They were slim fitting dark blue denim.

"These are the most popular jeans right now," said Harbinder. "I want you to sell lots of them. So try them on for me so you know how they fit."

Greta squeezed into the smallest size she could, wondering if her mother would have liked to know how tiny she was. Then she walked up and down modelling them for Harbinder.

"Good. Very good. Keep them on for the rest of the shift and sell as many as you can," he said.

Greta felt proud that she had been asked to wear their latest style of jeans at work. At the same time, she knew that Harbinder was in his office watching. Greta sold several pairs of the new jeans that day by showing them off to customers.

"These are the newest fashion," she'd say.

"They fit so good and are amazingly comfortable. If you tell me your size, I can get you a pair to try on," she pitched.

Most people wanted to try them because they looked good on Greta and they believed her when she told them they looked good on them too, even if they weren't flattering on all body types.

As it neared closing time, Greta took out the vacuum cleaner and started passing it through the change rooms while Jenna hung up people's try-ons. There were no more customers in the store and they would soon be locking up and counting the cash.

Harbinder came out from the back and arranged three chairs so they were facing each other.

Sitting in one of them, he said, "When you finished, come here girls."

"What's up?" Greta whispered to Jenna as they finalized the cash totals and closed up the bank deposit bag.

"I dunno," answered Jenna.

They brought the deposit bag to Harbinder.

"Have a seat. Both of you," he said.

They sat down and looked at each other.

"I saw you made some really good sales today. It was good teamwork," he continued.

He pulled out a bottle of Scotch from a paper bag that was beside him on the floor. He had three clear plastic glasses.

"We should celebrate," he said as he filled a glass about one third full and passed it to Jenna.

He did the same for Greta and finally poured one, a quarter full for himself.

He raised his glass and said, "Congratulations on an excellent week!"

"Cheers," they said to one another taking a sip of the smooth premium drink.

They chatted for a while over the glass of Scotch and he refilled the girls glasses a little more than he had on the first round. It was a very warming alcohol.

"Not too much for me," he laughed. "I'm driving."

Jenna and Greta finished their drinks.

"Now I drive you home," said Harbinder.

"Oh that's ok. I can walk," said Greta.

"I'm fine taking the subway," said Jenna.

"Nonsense," said Harbinder. "I have a beautiful car just waiting to chauffeur two beautiful girls home."

They all got up, tossed their empty cups into a waste basket, turned out the lights and processed to the rear exit of the store.

"Follow me," said Harbinder.

Jenna and Greta were both tipsy and giggly, easily impressed by the fancy car.

"Get in Jenna," he said as he opened the back door of his Mercedes.

"Greta, you sit in the front seat with me," he said.

As Harbinder got in and started the engine, he pulled out the bottle of Scotch and passed it back to Jenna.

"Help yourself if you want another drink," he said.

Behind the store was a concrete lane. Harbinder backed out slowly and got out onto the street.

"What's your address, Jenna?" he asked. "I forgot."

"Oh, it's 265 Carpenter Street. You have to turn right here," said Jenna as she swigged straight from the bottle.

"Oh yes. Now I remember," said Harbinder.

After about fifteen or twenty minutes of driving north on Young, Jenna said, "Turn right, up here."

The blinker clicked as Harbinder slowed the car, preparing to turn.

"Here?" he asked.

"Yup! Turn right and the first building on the left," Jenna said in a loud voice.

Harbinder pulled up in front of the tall apartment building. Jenna passed the bottle to Greta. Greta took the bottle as both she and Harbinder turned their heads to say good night to Jenna. She slammed the door shut and staggered towards the well-lit entrance of the apartment building.

As Harbinder drove away he locked the doors with the driver's control.

Greta pulled out a cigarette and asked, "You mind if I smoke?"

"Go ahead," said Harbinder.

Greta tried to open her window with a button on the door.

"Oh, I'll get that for you," said Harbinder as he used the driver's control.

"How's that?" he asked.

"Fine," answered Greta.

She took a drink from the bottle which was down about three quarters by now. She blew smoke and flicked her ashes out the window watching the big city buildings go by.

"What's your address?" Harbinder asked.

"You know where McCluskey's is?" Greta asked.

"Yes," answered Harbinder.

"I'm just behind there," said Greta.

"Ok," replied Harbinder.

It was quiet for a while and Harbinder drove rather slowly. He brushed Greta's knee with a sweeping hand.

"Those jeans look very nice on you," he said.

"Oh! I forgot to change back into my own jeans," Greta quickly responded.

"Don't worry," answered Harbinder. "You should wear them to work all of the time. It makes good sales."

"Oh no, I can't afford them," Greta froze momentarily. "I have to give them back."

"A beautiful girl like you should have nice things," said Harbinder. He placed the palm of his hand on Greta's knee saying, "I want you to have them."

"Oh no," said Greta. "I couldn't."

"You are so beautiful," said Harbinder. "I would like to take you out for dinner some time."

"But you are married," said Greta as she pulled her leg away, crossing it over the other.

"My wife doesn't need to know," he replied.

"We're almost there," said Greta, changing the subject and pointing ahead to the lit up sign of McCluskey's.

"You can let me out in front of McCluskey's," said Greta.

"Oh no. I am a gentleman and will take you to your door," said Harbinder.

"Then turn left on the next street," she pointed.

"Okay," he responded, slowing down and switching on the blinker.

"Then the first street on the right," continued Greta.

Harbinder followed Greta's directions and drove slower, eventually pulling up in front of the house where Greta lived.

"Look, I didn't mean anything by it," said Harbinder. "You are just such a pretty girl, and you should have nice things."

"That's ok," said Greta nervously reaching for the door handle.

She pulled on it but the door was still locked and under his control. He stared at her.

"Let me know if there is anything I can do for you. I could take good care of you. Keep the jeans," he reiterated as he reached over and caressed her cheek softly.

She heard the door unlock.

"Have a good night," he said.

She quickly opened the door and got out.

"Good night," she said.

Harbinder watched Greta walk down the driveway until she disappeared from view, then drove off.

Greta hated going back to the apartment. She cautiously unlocked the door. Slowly opening it, she turned on the light to make sure no one was inside waiting for her. She pushed the loveseat in front of the door and lit a candle and placed it on the counter to kill the dank air.

She went back to the letter from Jeff.

Dear Greta, Thank you for the letter you sent. I wasn't expecting it, so it was a pleasant surprise. I know you've only been gone for a few weeks, but it feels like much longer. I hope things are good with you. It must be exciting to be in the big city. I'm working and saving money. I miss hanging out with you, like smoking a few and drinking, and just hanging out or going for walks together. It's not the same here without you. I told you already that Brenda and Mark hooked up and that she's pregnant. They didn't want to get married or anything but they moved in together and are getting ready for the baby. I can't imagine having a baby at our age. I still see them once in a while but it's way different now that they are a couple and starting a family.
Maybe when you get time you can write me again and let me know how you're doing. Or call me sometime if that's easier. It'd be good to hear your voice.

There's a long weekend next month, maybe I can take a day off before and after and come to see you. That's if you want. Anyway, just wanted to let you know that I'm thinking about you. I love the letter you sent. I keep reading it over and over again so I can imagine your voice in my head. I really miss you a lot and I hope I can come to see you soon.
Your friend always.
With Love.
Jeff

Taking a deep breath, Greta went to the bathroom and looked in the mirror. She fixed her hair and makeup and dabbed herself with Anais Anais perfume. She blew out the candle, put on her black pumps, and pushed the loveseat away from the door. She marched up to McCluskey's. The Scotch had just warmed her up and she didn't want to be alone and she didn't want to lose the buzz she had going.

It was jazz night and the music could be heard halfway down the block. As Greta came out the other end of the catwalk onto Main Street, she turned left towards the booming music. There were people standing outside smoking weed and laughing in small groups reminiscent of the high school smoking area cliques. Greta weaved her way through them and waltzed into a packed jazzy scene.

She stood as tall as she could as if she was looking for someone. She didn't see Cory or Graham. The old man usually at the end of the bar wasn't there either. And as Greta shimmied her way up to the crowded bar it was a different bartender.

He shouted, "What'll you have?"

"A Canadian," Greta shouted back.

She knew from before what it cost and placed the money, tip included, on the bar when the bottle of beer arrived.

"No glass, thanks," she said.

She grabbed the bottle and took a big swig. There were no empty seats at the bar and no empty tables. Many people were standing and roaming as the loud conversations mixed with the music, individual voices indiscernible. She stood beside a support beam. A good looking middle-aged man came up to her.

"Hello. Are you alone?" he asked.

"Yes," she said while watching the band.

"Do you come here often?" he asked.

"Sometimes," answered Greta.

"Oh, I've never seen you here before," he continued. "My name's Martin."

"Greta," she replied.

As she avoided looking at him, she caught the stern leer of Daryl, who was across the room at a standup table. Greta tensed up and turned her attention to Martin, trying to make it appear like they were together.

She stood a little closer to him and said, "I've never seen you here before either. It's kinda loud here, maybe there's someplace quieter we can go to talk."

"Sure. Let's get outta here," he replied.

Daryl was still staring at Greta as she slipped her hand under Martin's arm and marched towards the exit. As they walked out onto the sidewalk, Greta pulled out a cigarette.

"Here. Let me light that for you," he said as he flicked his lighter.

"Thanks," said Greta catching a whiff of marijuana.

"I wish I had something stronger to smoke," she said.

"Oh, well I've got some stuff back at my apartment," said Martin. "It's only a couple of blocks from here."

Wanting to urgently get as far away from Daryl as possible, Greta replied, "Let's go!"

He had a really nice apartment in a building close to Young Street. He invited Greta in and made her a strong but palatable fancy looking cocktail in a blender with ice. It was like drinking a slushy and went down as easily. Martin also had some fine hashish that he placed in a water pipe that cooled the sensation of the smoke so there was no burn on the throat. They sat on the couch smoking and talking.

Sometime the next morning Greta woke up with her face smushed up against a pillow on Martin's couch. She slowly rolled off and pushed herself up to a standing position. Then she headed to the bathroom holding onto the walls as they swayed. Lifting the toilet seat, she began to hurl the pink concoction from the night before. She rinsed with mouthwash she found under the vanity and dampened the corner of a towel to wipe away the raccoon marks from under her eyes. She couldn't call a cab because she didn't know where she was. So she quietly left the apartment while Martin snored with his bedroom door half open.

Once she was outside, she surmised by the density and flow of the traffic where Young Street was and walked in that direction. Once she got to Young, she was able to hail a cab.

She entered her apartment cautiously and moved the loveseat in front of the door. The rest of that day and the next were spent recovering from her hangover.

Chapter 11
Bible Camp

There was a knock at the door on Tuesday morning.

"Who is it?!" Greta loudly queried.

"Charlie! I have your mail," he replied pleasantly.

"Just leave it outside the door," Greta said, with scissors in her hand.

She'd used them to cut her hair, slept with them, and carried them in her purse ever since the night he raped her. She held them firmly and was ready to use them.

"But I have something else too," he said. "I can't leave it outside."

"What is it?" asked Greta.

"A gift," he said. "Can you please open the door so I can give it to you?"

Greta pushed the loveseat aside and unlocked the door. She held the scissors concealed behind the left side of her body as she opened the door only a crack. He stood there, straight and tall, freshly showered, shaved and neatly dressed. He held two envelopes in one hand and a basket of fruit was nestled like a baby in his arm.

"Here's your mail," he said, handing her the envelopes.

She took it with her right hand, folded it, and stuffed it into the pocket of her baggy sweatpants. She had not started getting ready for work yet and wasn't wearing makeup. Her hair was clean but not styled.

"You look lovely today," he smiled softly.

"This is for you," he added as he held out the fruit basket.

She opened the door just enough to grab the handle of the basket and place it on the floor inside the apartment. She stared coldly, straight into Charlie's eyes. Her youthful, naive beauty was dead. It had been hardened into defensive loathing, projected in scorn.

"Thanks," she said sarcastically.

He stepped back and Greta slammed the door shut.

While drinking an instant coffee and smoking a cigarette, Greta did her makeup with black eyeliner and mascara, rouged cheeks, and red lip liner and lipstick. She was still hiding the bare patch on the crown of her head with curls, teasing, and hairspray. She pinned up what she could before heading to Joe's. It was a cool day, so she covered her uniform with a camel trench coat.

She arrived at work early so she could have a cigarette and coffee while looking through the newspaper for vacant apartments. She needed something cheap and close to work so she could get away from Charlie, but there was nothing suitable and affordable. Joe popped out of the kitchen and handed her a message.

"There was a call for you," he said.

It was from Dr. Pigeon's office.

Greta went to the payphone and dialed nervously. Her worst fear was confirmed. She was pregnant. They asked her to come to see the doctor again and she took an appointment for Friday at eleven. Her face flushed and she began to tremble. Hanging up the phone, Greta ran to the back room, holding back tears. She looked in the mirror and tucked some loose hairs into a hairnet, powdered her nose, took a deep breath and prepared to start her shift. All she could think about was getting an abortion, and that kept her going.

Connie could tell that Greta was upset and had noticed the recent changes in her personality and appearance.

"Is everything ok?" she asked.

"Oh yeah. I'm fine," said Greta shaking her head.

"Let me know if there's anything you wanna talk about. I'm always here for you, you know," said Connie.

"Thanks Connie, but I'm fine. Really," Greta lied.

"Ok dear," replied Connie. "But here's my number if you ever need to talk. Anytime."

She handed Greta a small piece of paper with her name and number on it. Greta tucked it in her bra.

"Thanks," she managed a smile.

Greta tried to remain cheerful with her customers. Darlene didn't bother Greta with any questions about her more sullen demeanor and they just worked alongside each other efficiently.

"Hey. I never told you before, but I really like your new hairstyle. Very modern," Darlene stated genuinely.

"Thanks. I just needed a change," Greta smiled with gratitude.

"Oh for sure. I get that," Darlene replied, always with her funky earrings and brusk confidence.

Greta lightened up a bit when the bells chimed and Cory and Graham appeared.

"Oh those two again," said Darlene with a chuckle. "You may as well show them a table because they'll want you to wait on them."

Greta approached them with menus and a fresh pot of coffee.

"You can take this booth," Greta said. "It's all set."

"Perfect," said Cory. "The usual will be fine."

"The usual it is... pastrami on rye and a BLT. Coming right up!"

She filled their coffee cups and walked away with the menus. Then she kept herself busy with cleaning, trying to avoid talking to them but she had no other customers. When she brought them their food she also brought a basket of fries.

"Some extra fries for you to share. On the house," she said.

"Sweet," said Graham, as Greta tried to walk away.

"Hey," said Cory. "Don't go away so fast."

Greta stopped and stared at Cory who was looking especially handsome with his clean tousled locks and chocolate brown eyes.

"It's been a while. How 'bout coming to McCluskey's with us tonight?" he asked.

"I didn't bring a change of clothes," said Greta. "I couldn't go there dressed like this."

"We could swing by your place first so you can change if you want," said Cory.

"Do you guys want some dessert?" asked Greta, changing the subject. "We've still got some scrumptious strawberry shortcake and some peach cobbler I'd highly recommend."

"I'll have the peach cobbler," said Graham.

"Yeah, yeah, same here. We're cobbler gobblers," Cory snickered.

"You're lame," said Graham.

But they all snickered anyway.

"What about tonight?" Cory asked.

He reached out to touch Greta's free hand. Greta didn't pull away. She reluctantly accepted his touch.

"Ok. I'll be through here in about forty-five minutes. But at ten o'clock we lock the door and you'll have to wait outside for me," she said.

She brought their desserts, the cheque, and each a take-out coffee to drink outside while they waited for her. The men were happy to stand around outside smoking cigarettes, chatting and drinking their coffees while they waited for Greta to sweep.

Darlene, seeing that Greta's suitors were waiting for her said, "You go ahead. I can finish up here."

"Are you sure?" Greta asked.

"Yes. Yes. Go ahead. I'm just going to wipe down the counter and the backbar," Darlene reassured. "Have a good night."

"You're the best Darlene," said Greta. "I'll see you tomorrow."

The men greeted Greta with enthusiasm as they began walking towards McCluskey's. She plunged her hands into the deep pockets of her trench coat to keep warm. They reached the catwalk.

"Why don't you go ahead and grab us a table while I go with Greta?" Cory said.

"Yeah sure," Graham replied. "See ya in a bit."

Cory placed his hand on Greta's shoulder while they walked down the catwalk but Greta did not reciprocate in any way, keeping her hands in her pockets.

"Is everything ok?" he asked.

"Yeah. Fine," said Greta. "It'll be good to just sit down and have a beer. It's been a long day."

"Musta been, especially on your feet," said Cory.

As they approached Greta's apartment, Cory was going to follow her inside.

"Wait outside. It's a mess in here," she said.

Taken aback, Cory replied, "Oh. Ok."

"I'll only be a minute," said Greta.

She nearly tripped on the fruit basket that was left on the floor by the door. She picked it up and put it on the counter before quickly stripping off her uniform and tossing it on a stool. She put on a worn pair of old jeans and a grey knit sweater that hugged her curves. Sliding into her pumps, she tossed on a jean jacket and hurried out to the door.

"See, it didn't take long," said Greta. "Let's go!"

"Ok," he answered, catching up to her hurried pace.

"You look great by the way," said Cory.

"Thanks," replied Greta.

"I really like the new hairstyle," he added. "Looks sophisticated and modern. Makes you look older too."

"Thanks," she replied again.

Cory grabbed Greta's hand saying, "Hold up."

Greta stopped, "Yeah? What?"

"About that night," he started. "It was really great."

"Oh. That. Yeah. It was great for me too," she replied unenthusiastically.

"I was worried that we didn't use any protection," said Cory. "I'll make sure I have a condom with me from now on."

"Okay," she replied.

"Good then. I just wanted to make sure you were ok with that," he said.

"Well, that's if there is a next time," she giggled flirtatiously.

"I hope so," he said as he pinched her waist. "You know you're hot."

"Oh really," said Greta. "Well, thank you."

They walked the rest of the way to McCluskey's holding hands but once they entered the bar Greta let go and headed straight towards the table where Graham was waiting for them. The waitress approached as they sat down.

"What can I get for you?" she asked.

"I'll start with a screwdriver please," said Greta.

"I'll have a rum and coke," said Cory.

"Another pitcher of draft and two more glasses for the table. And a whiskey, neat," said Graham.

The festivities began with Graham dropping the shot glass of whiskey into his glass of beer. It made a splash and he chugged the whole thing down at once. The shot glass plunked hard back into the glass when it was set on the table. They all laughed.

They played pool, drank, and took turns going outside in pairs to smoke joints.

Greta completely forgot about being pregnant and went home alone that night. She'd already told herself she was getting rid of it anyway, so why think about it?

The basket of fruit was an ominous reminder of her situation. There was a card taped to the basket. It read:

You are as sweet as a freshly plucked fruit. Love, Charles.

Greta was sickened by his words and threw the card in the trash. She shoved the loveseat in front of the door, had a hot shower and went to bed with her hair wrapped in a towel, holding the scissors in her hand.

The next day, she took the fruit basket with her when she left for Joe's Coffee House. There was a beggar seated on the ground near a big church on Main Street. She approached him and made eye contact. Greta held out the fruit basket.

"This is for you," she said.

The man's faded blue eyes sparkled and then welled with held back tears of gratitude.

"Oh my. God bless you dear," he said.

She j-walked across the street to get to a liquor store where she bought a bottle of cheap wine and a mickey of cheap vodka. The clerk inserted each into its own paper bag that she put into her backpack. Then she headed to Joe's for an unremarkable shift. She thought about the new letters from Jeff and Myra.

After work, she approached her apartment door with the usual caution, keys in one hand and scissors in the other. Slowly opening the door, she pushed it fully wide to make sure Charlie wasn't hiding behind it.

She was startled by a voice behind her.

"Good evening Greta."

Turning quickly, she tightened her grip on the scissors. It was Charlie looming over her.

Seeing her reaction, he said, "Oh, I didn't mean to startle you."

"What do you want?" she asked.

"I came to see about the rent," said Charlie. "I didn't get a cheque for next month yet."

"Oh," said Greta. "I thought I was paid up until the end of November?"

"November's cheque was cancelled. It bounced," said Charlie.

"Oh," said Greta. "I didn't know. I haven't got it right now."

"Well," said Charlie. "It's due on the 1st. But if you don't have the money, we could make other arrangements."

He moved in closer to Greta.

"No! I'll get you the money soon," she said adamantly as she slammed the door.

She quickly locked it and blocked it with the loveseat. She knew if he really wanted to get in he had a key and the strength to push the loveseat out of the way.

"Have a good night sweetie," he laughed through the door.

Taking a deep breath, Greta put down her backpack and purse, and laid the scissors and keys on the counter. Pouring warm wine into a short glass, Greta reached for the unopened bent letters from Jeff and Myra. Wanting to get the discomfort of reading her mother's words out of the way, she used the scissors to slit open that letter first. It read:

Dear Greta, I hope you are well. I was able to get a partial refund on your tuition and cancelled the rest of the post-dated rent cheques. It will help cover some of the long-distance charges you've made on my account. I hope you are happy with the choice you made and learn to save your money and spend it wisely. When you have time, you should go to church, maybe you will find something inspirational there in the music, or the preacher's words. Even the architecture and art in the churches can be inspiring. Just a suggestion since your dad has been finding it helpful to connect with our pastor and a men's group.

Church just made her think of the time when her mother sent her to Bible Camp. She was thirteen. The girls slept in rustic log cabins with bunks. The camp was on a small lake and there was a common building for gatherings and meals. Greta was in a study group that was led by a young adult male seminary student named Calvin. She enjoyed the philosophical teachings and discussions that happened in his group. He definitely had charisma.

There was a lunch break and it was a gorgeous sunny day. Calvin and Greta started a conversation while the others dispersed. They touched on life and death and the vastness of the universe. The mature topic held Greta's interest and she enjoyed the richly poetic and ethereal answers Calvin provided. He asked her if she wanted to go for a walk around the lake since it was so nice out.

Halfway around the lake, Calvin suggested they take a break and enjoy the sun and the majestic view. They sat in a clearing on a large rock and Calvin leaned in towards Greta, put his hands on her and tried to kiss her. Greta jumped up and ran back to the camp, leaving Calvin behind. She did not return to the study group he led for the duration of the camp. She was violated by someone she was supposed to trust and respect.

She lit a cigarette and downed the entirety of that first glass of warm wine. Filling it a second time, she finished reading the letter from Myra.

If you change your mind about school, there are other options and different courses and different schools we could look at. But it's up to you. Let us know if you change your mind. Call or write soon to let us know how you are doing. Love, Mom

Loneliness enveloped her as a tear rolled down her cheek. She opened the letter from Jeff. It read:

Hi Greta, I've been thinking about you a lot lately. You must be busy, like me, with working two jobs and everything. I was thinking about coming to see you. Remembrance Day is on a Thursday, so I can take the Friday and Monday off and make a 5 day weekend to come and see you. I hope that works for you because I've already told my boss and my work buddy can give me a ride down because he's got family down there he is planning to visit. Can't wait to see you!!
Friends forever, lotsa Love, Jeff

She missed how much Jeff understood her. With that, she put the half empty wine bottle and the mickey of vodka under the sink behind the coin jar and took a hot shower. In only a t-shirt and panties, she curled up in bed with the scissors in her hand.

Chapter 12
The Blue Velvet Curtain

Greta wore the jeans her boss gave her on her next shift at Jeans N Tops. When she arrived, he asked her to work in the office at the start of her shift. It seemed counterintuitive if she was wearing the jeans to boost sales.

She entered the office and sat down at the desk that faced the two-way mirror. She felt like they were spying on Jenna as she assisted a customer.

Greta looked down at the ledger, cheque book, and pile of invoices.

"Let me know if you have any questions," he said.

For each bill Greta made a corresponding cheque and entered the data into the ledger with the cheque and invoice numbers associated with each payment. He pulled his chair close to Greta's and watched over her shoulder.

"Mmm... You smell very nice," he said.

"It must be the vanilla shampoo I use," said Greta.

"Do you like the jeans? It is nice to see you wearing them again," said Harbinder.

"Yeah," said Greta. "I like them. Thanks."

Whenever Greta made a cheque for something, she'd give it to her boss for approval and signature. He kept close track of what Greta did and rarely left the room.

He said, "I have an appointment with my eye doctor and will be back in about an hour. When you are done that stack of papers, you can go help Jenna until I get back."

"That's fine," replied Greta.

After he left, she took a piece of lightweight paper and placed it over one of Harbinder's signatures and carefully traced it. She repeated this a couple of times, specifically looking for a copy of his signature that was made with a dark pen and lots of pressure so it would show through the paper better. She had copied her mother's signature and mastered it for sicknotes back in high school so she figured she could use the same technique for her boss's signature. She then carefully removed a blank cheque from the cheque book. She took the next one in sequence so that it would be less obvious that one had been removed. She placed the blank cheque and the traced signatures in an envelope and slid it under her camisole, against her skin. Then she made sure she finished the pile of invoices and receipts, cross referencing and filing the receipts and leaving the invoices with matching cheques for her boss to sign neatly on top of the ledger book. Before joining Jenna on the sales floor she took the envelope out from under her camisole and placed it carefully in her purse.

"He's gone to the eye doctor's," she told Jenna.

"Oh. Ok. That's good. He hardly ever leaves," Jenna replied. "How's it going back there?" she asked.

"Honestly, it's awful. That room is so small. It's claustrophobic," said Greta.

"I'm glad he doesn't ask me to work in the office," said Jenna.

"Yeah. You lucked out," Greta replied.

"I'm not his type," said Jenna.

"Eew, he's not my type," Greta retorted.

They laughed quietly and continued working.

When Harbinder returned he asked Greta back to the office where she showed him the cheques that needed to be signed.

"Can you take them to the post office now?" he asked.

"Sure," Greta replied. "It's almost dinner time. How 'bout I take you out for something to eat when you get back?"

"Oh, no," answered Greta. "That wouldn't be right. I'm working."

"It's ok," said Harbinder. "You will still get paid."

"No," said Greta. "It's not just that. You are married."

"My wife doesn't need to know," said Harbinder.

"No," said Greta, again. "I would prefer not."

"Ok," said Harbinder. "Whatever you want. I can order the food to eat here. There is a Greek place just up the street. You like souvlaki?"

"I've never had it so I don't know," said Greta.

"I will order that and some salads. You can pick it up after you go to the post office," said Harbinder.

"Alright," said Greta, politely.

"I'll call now and place the order while you place the cheques in the envelopes," said Harbinder.

He picked up the phone to place the order. Then he pulled out a bundle of bills held together with a fancy clip. He peeled off a couple of large bills and handed them to Greta.

"You know where the post office is and Apollos is about two blocks south from here. You can't miss it," he said.

"Bring back the change," he added as Greta stood up.

She got her jacket, grabbed her purse, and walked past Jenna who was behind the cash register putting through a sale. Jenna and Greta's eyes met as she passed. It was as if for a moment they were reading each other's minds.

"I'm just going to the post office and getting something to eat," said Greta. "I won't be long."

"Ok hon," answered Jenna.

She crossed the street at the intersection to get to the post office. Before seeing the cashier for stamps, she went to the public washroom and locked herself in a stall. There were no outward signs that she was pregnant. In fact, she was thinner than ever. She touched up her lipstick and hair in the mirror, then went to get stamps.

She lit a cigarette as soon as she exited the post office and kept going in search of Apollos restaurant. The order for Jeans N Tops was ready when she arrived.

Back at the store, Greta asked Jenna if she'd had her break yet.

"No. But no worries. Whenever," said Jenna.

"I'll try to get out of the back soon so you can have supper," said Greta.

"Ok. I understand," answered Jenna, looking into Greta's eyes knowingly.

Greta entered the office to find Harbinder sitting back in a chair with his turban off. His long black and grey hair was pulled over to one side. He had placed a small table in front of himself and another chair across from him.

"Oh good. You're back," he said.

"Have a seat," he gestured.

Greta sat down and placed the paper bag on the table. Harbinder tore open the bag and pulled out the containers, paper plates, napkins and plastic utensils.

"I hope you like this," he said. "It is very good."

Greta said nothing as Harbinder assembled two plates with a little of everything on each.

"The tzatziki sauce is especially good," said Harbinder. "They make it fresh."

"Mmm, it smells good," Greta tried to be polite as he passed her a plate.

She took a forkful of rice and nibbled on the chicken souvlaki. Harbinder ate hurriedly, then reached in a cabinet beside him for a bottle of wine and two tumblers. He filled them halfway and passed one to Greta.

"A toast to our first dinner together," he said.

She raised her glass and took a guilty sip. She wanted the wine but was repulsed by the man.

He added, "Next time, I hope you will let me take you out some place nice."

Greta faked a smile, took another mouthful of rice and drank the warm red wine.

Pulling her words together she said, "Well, like I said, it wouldn't be right."

"You worry too much," said Harbinder. "I promise, my wife will never know."

Then after a moment of silence, Harbinder filled their wine glasses again and gazed at Greta.

"You are so beautiful," he said.

She faked another smile and thanked him. Then he slipped the shoe off of his left foot and stretched his long leg under the small table and stroked the inside of her leg. Greta jolted back but there wasn't far she could go in the cramped room. Her chair hit the wall.

"What's the matter?" he asked.

"Jenna needs to take her break," answered Greta as she got up and left the room in a nervous sweat.

She took a deep breath and walked out onto the sales floor towards Jenna. Her state of panic was obvious and she was visibly flushed.

Jenna asked, "Are you alright?"

As her heart pounded Greta answered, "Yes, you can take your break now."

Jenna agreed and left Greta alone.

Greta took another deep breath and approached a customer who was browsing through the racks.

"Is there anything I can help you with?" she asked her.

"No thanks," the woman smiled. "I'm just browsing."

"No problem," replied Greta. "Let me know if you need me to find your size in anything."

The woman thanked her again and as she turned around a familiar face entered the store.

"Martin!" she exclaimed. "What a surprise to see you."

Martin was better looking than Greta remembered. And he was neatly dressed.

"I wasn't quite sure if this was the right place you said you worked at," said Martin.

"I don't recall telling you where I worked. Did you come to shop?" she asked.

"I'm not surprised you don't remember some things from that night," Martin smiled. "I'm looking for a pair of jeans. Could you help me out?"

"It would be my pleasure," she said. "Are you looking for a stone wash, a dark dyed denim? What's your preference?"

"I'd be happy to entertain any suggestions you might have," he said with a genuine air of sophistication.

"Great!" she said. "Let me show you a couple of our newest styles I think you might like."

Keeping busy with Martin took her mind off Harbinder's advance. Jenna returned from her break, and soon after their employer emerged with his hair wrapped back into his turban.

"You girls can close up," he said. "I'll see you tomorrow."

"Ok," said Greta, with fake cheerfulness. "No problem."

He did not acknowledge Greta. After spending at least an hour trying on lots of jeans and tops, Martin bought a pair of jeans and a sweater.

"I am going to a little spot up the street for a drink. If you want, I can meet you back here when you get off. If you'd like to join me?" said Martin as he was paying.

"Sounds good. I get off in an hour," Greta replied.

Jenna and Greta finished out the rest of their shift with minimal discussion but a sense of camaraderie. The deposit bag went into a slot that dropped into an in-store safe and Jenna locked up with a key for the front door. Martin was waiting outside at the appointed time.

"Can we walk you to your stop?" he asked Jenna.

"Ah, it's only a block and a half up that way to the subway," she replied.

"We're going in that direction anyway," said Martin.

"Great then," she said.

They walked together until they got to the stairs leading down to the subway.

"This is it," she said. "It was nice meeting you. Hope you enjoy your evening."

"Good night," said Greta.

Martin added, "Nice meeting you too!"

Greta and Martin walked another two blocks and turned left until they arrived at a blue neon sign that read Saffire Lounge. The entrance opened into a long dimly lit hallway. They passed a coat check window and public washrooms before coming to a blue velvet curtain. Through it was a large bouncer.

"Hi Frankie," Martin said to the man.

"Evening," he replied with his arms folded across his chest.

Frankie relaxed and held the curtain back for them. The dark room was carpeted in sapphire blue with plushy upholstered booths along the walls. There was a grand piano on one side of a small dance floor and a strobe light twirling above. There was an older gentleman tinkling the ivories softly, and a large deep glass bowl with coins and bills sitting atop the piano for tips.

Greta tucked her hand under Martin's arm as he led her towards an empty booth.

"It's not too busy here on Thursday nights," said Martin. "But the music and atmosphere are good."

"It's very nice," said Greta.

When the waitress came over, Martin said, "How about a margarita?"

"Sounds good," Greta replied.

There was a large ashtray in the middle of the table and Greta offered Martin a cigarette.

"Thanks," he said as he pulled a lighter from his pocket and passed the flame to Greta before lighting his own cigarette.

For a moment she actually felt safe. She relaxed and let the nicotine kick in as the tension flowed out of her body. The gentle piano music was more comforting than she expected it would be.

"You know, I used to play the piano," said Greta.

"Really?" responded Martin. "Well I'm not surprised that you are both beautiful and talented. You don't play anymore?"

"No. And I'm not talented," said Greta. "My mom just made me take lessons."

"I stand corrected. Then you are beautiful and learned," Martin replied.

"That's sweet of you to say," she said. "But I cannot take credit for my looks either, that's genetic."

"Whatever reason you are the way you are makes no difference to me, dear Greta," said Martin. "What I see in you, is precisely the reason you are here."

"What do you mean?" she asked.

"Do you recall my telling you about my work that night we first met?" he asked.

"Vaguely. You said you're an artist," said Greta.

"Well yes, that's right," said Martin. "But did I mention that our private group meets for figure drawing classes at the College?"

"No. I don't recall that. Honestly, I don't recall much about that night," said Greta. "I don't even remember telling you where I work. I'm sorry."

"No need to apologize. I understand," continued Martin with a chuckle. "We were both rather inebriated that evening."

"Did I tell you that I work at Joe's Coffee House too?" she asked.

"If you did. I don't remember. So I guess there are a few things I don't remember either," said Martin.

"Those drinks you made in the blender were so yummy. And so is this margarita," she said.

"It was one of my famous Hawaiian punch concoctions, with lots of vodka and ice. Always a hit," he said.

Greta raised her glass to Martin as he reciprocated the gesture. She found him quite charming. The waitress looked over as they were finishing their margaritas and Martin motioned with his finger and a nod that they would each have another. When she returned with their drinks, she wiped down the table, dumped their ashtray and placed fresh cardboard coasters under their glasses. She placed a little cocktail napkin in front of each of them.

"We have an amazing chocolate cheesecake tonight if you're interested," she said.

"How about it Greta?" asked Martin.

"Sounds delicious," said Greta.

"Bring us one piece and two forks," said Martin with a wink at the waitress.

"You got it Martin," she replied with smiling familiarity.

"So, I wanted to tell you more about the art I do," he said.

Then he paused and relaxed back into the cushioned booth, sipping on the margarita. There was something worldly about him.

"Our group is always looking for new models," he said. "Would you be interested in posing? We pay well."

"Really?" asked Greta. "What would I need to do?"

"Well, we usually start with a few short poses of two or three minutes each that express natural movement as a warm-up," he explained. "Then we like a few longer poses up to twenty or thirty minutes in length. But only what feels natural and comfortable for you."

"Oh," said Greta. "I think I could do that."

"Good," smiled Martin. "What is your availability?"

"I'm off Sunday and Monday," answered Greta.

"We can use you on Sunday afternoon then," said Martin. "From one until four."

Greta asked how she would be paid. Martin told her she'd be paid in cash before class started and where to show up. He also explained that it was her choice to pose either draped or undraped and that undraped paid twice what draped paid.

"Thanks Martin," said Greta. "I could use the extra dough since I'm looking for a new place to live."

"Ah... Ok," said Martin. "Well I hope this will help." They ate the decadent chocolate cheesecake and followed that with Spanish coffees. When they left, Martin hailed a cab and told the driver to drop Greta off first.

As soon as she got out of the cab, Greta slipped her hand into her bag and pulled out her scissors. Looking all around in case Charlie was lurking about she entered her apartment and turned on the light. She checked behind her bed, in the closet, behind the counter, and in the bathroom before sliding the loveseat in front of the door. Then she read the letter from Jeff again, took a hot steamy shower, and curled up under the covers with a towel wrapped around her freshly washed hair. As she thought about the modelling job she fell asleep clutching the scissors in her hand.

Chapter 13
The Nurse's Glare

Her alarm clock went off. Everything was the way she remembered it before falling asleep, scissors still in her hand. She slapped the alarm off, sat up and remembered her doctor's appointment was that morning. She popped out of bed and put the kettle on, brushed her teeth, and waited for the curling iron to heat up.

Her hair had lots of volume from having gone to bed with it wrapped in a towel. The towel came undone during the night and it was completely dry. She applied foundation over her whole face and picked out a couple of knots from her hair. Step by step, she applied the rest of her makeup and strategically curled and sprayed every strand of her hair before teasing and arranging it to hide the bald patch. There was only a slight bit of new growth. She checked it over and over in the mirrors until she was satisfied there was no evidence of the bald patch showing through.

She would have to go straight to work at Jeans N Tops after her doctor's appointment. So she put on an older pair of jeans with a sweater that hugged her curves. Leaving the bathroom light on, Greta left, locking the door behind her.

When she arrived at the doctor's office, she waited only a short time before the nurse asked her to be seated in the doctor's private office. The nurse had her clipboard again and asked more questions. When was your last period? Are you in a relationship? Have you started taking prenatal vitamins? Do you smoke cigarettes? Do you drink alcohol?

Greta blurted out, "I want an abortion."

"Well, we don't do that here," said the nurse rudely. "But we can refer you to a clinic."

"That's fine," said Greta. "I want a referral then."

"Well first," said the nurse. "There are a few more things we will need to discuss with you so that you are making an informed decision."

Greta was silent while the nurse explained that it was possible to give the baby up for adoption if she did not terminate the pregnancy. She also asked if the father knew about the pregnancy because he might want to be involved in childrearing and support.

"Ok," said Greta. "Those are not possibilities for me. I understand and I want the referral please."

The nurse told Greta to wait and the doctor would be right in to see her. When Dr. Pigeon entered the room he had a serious demeanor and sat imposingly in the large armchair behind his desk.

"So, you are a little over six weeks along," said Dr. Pigeon. "You know if you don't want the baby, there are many people who can't have children that are waiting to adopt."

"I don't think I could go through the pregnancy," said Greta. "That would be too hard."

"Is the father in the picture?" asked the doctor.

"No," said Greta. "The father doesn't know."

"Don't you think you should talk to the father about it and see what he wants?" asked the doctor.

"Well, we aren't together," said Greta.

"Maybe he would support the baby and be involved," said the doctor.

"No," said Greta. "I want an abortion. Please stop talking like there's a baby."

"Fine," the doctor said gruffly. "See the receptionist and she will give you a referral appointment to the clinic. We do not deal with that here."

Greta got up, feeling demoralized and walked down the hall, passing the nurse's glare along the way to the receptionist.

"I need a referral," Greta said.

"Take a seat," she was told.

Dr. Pigeon entered the reception area and passed his instructions onto the receptionist regarding a referral for Greta. They stared at her in condescension and whispered. After a few moments, the receptionist called Greta's name and she approached the desk. She was handed a card with an appointment time and the address on it.

"Here you go dear," said the receptionist. "Don't miss this appointment because what you're doing is time sensitive."

"I understand," said Greta.

She took the card and went on her way to work. Jenna was happy to see Greta when she arrived. When she went to the back of the store to hang up her coat and change her shoes, Harbinder approached her.

"I have some bookkeeping for you to do," he said.

Greta turned around and said, "I won't be able to work in the office anymore."

Harbinder was taken aback and insulted by Greta's bold statement.

"After everything I've done for you, you tell me this?" he scoffed.

"I'm sorry. I'm just not comfortable working in the office. I would rather be on the floor helping customers," she replied.

With a beet red face he said, "We'll see about that."

Greta went out onto the sales floor. Jenna overheard everything. She was happy to have Greta by her side because she was overwhelmed trying to keep the store organized and help multiple customers on the cash and in the fitting rooms.

"I'm so glad you stood up to him," she said.

"We'll see how that goes. He wasn't too happy about it," said Greta, a little shaken.

"Screw him," Jenna whispered. "He sits back there watching us like a peeping Tom."

Knowing they were being watched, they separated and organized the entire store according to size, style, color, and price. There were discount racks to arrange and dusty shelves to clean. Harbinder came out from the back of the store wearing his overcoat.

"There's a new schedule at the back. Make sure you check it before leaving tonight. I'm leaving now," he said.

Jenna and Greta looked up from what they were doing and acknowledged what their boss had said, glancing at each other.

When they knew he had left the building, Jenna said, "I wonder what that's all about."

She went to the back room and returned with the schedule in hand. They looked at it together behind the cash counter and Greta saw immediately that her three regular eight hour shifts had been cut drastically. She now had only three hours each day on Thursday, Friday, and Saturday.

"I told you he was pissed," said Greta. "I can't survive on nine hours a week!"

"Yeah, he'll probably start interviewing new girls again," Jenna replied. "I'm so sorry. I really like working with you."

"Well, it's not your fault," Greta replied. "There's nothing you could do about it. And it's not fair."

Jenna and Greta finished out their shift and said good night after Jenna locked the front door. They went their separate ways. Walking through the catwalk at night no longer posed the ominous feeling of foreboding it had in the past. Her past trepidation was now reserved for approaching her apartment door. Key in one hand and scissors in the other, Greta's senses were on high alert. She looked for signs of Charlie outside and entered the apartment carefully. Opening the door fully, she turned on the light, and checked the few places he could possibly hide.

Taking a deep breath, the reality of losing more than half her pay from one job added another layer of complexity to her dire situation.

Greta gently brushed her hair and pulled it off her face with a headband. Then she took a few cotton balls and soaked them with baby oil to remove her makeup. Then she took a warm washcloth and removed the excess residue from her face, brushed her teeth and went to bed, with scissors in her hand.

She was startled awake by a loud banging on her door. She got up as the banging continued.

"I'm coming!" yelled Greta. "Just a second."

She put the scissors into the pocket of her baggy sweatpants and pushed the loveseat out of the way.

"Who is it?" she asked.

"It's me," answered Charlie through the door. "Your rent is past due!"

Greta panicked because she didn't have all the money. She opened the door slowly, squinting at the bright morning daylight.

"Oh. Gee Charlie," she started. "I haven't got the whole amount scraped together."

"Well you're already past due. I've been waiting," said Charlie. "What are you going to do about it!?"

"I could give you half," said Greta. "And pay the rest in a few days. It's just been a tough month."

Charlie rolled his eyes and said a long drawn out, "Well... I guess that would be ok... this time."

"I only have cash, so I'll need a receipt," Greta said.

Charlie pulled a receipt pad and pen from his inside coat pocket. Greta closed the door and after a minute came back with a handful of cash. She counted it out in front of him as he wrote out the receipt. They exchanged.

"I don't want you making a habit of this," said Charlie with a smirk. "If you can't pay up on time I will be looking for other compensation."

"It won't happen again," said Greta.

She closed the door, locked it, and slid the loveseat back in front of it.

Her new hours at Jeans N Tops had her starting at five so she took the opportunity to go to the laundromat before getting ready for work. Then she left early enough to swing by Joe's Coffee House where Connie was working with another part-time girl. Greta sat at the staff booth where Joe sat to count the cash at the end of the night.

Connie came over and said, "Hi hon. Can I get you a coffee?"

"I can get it myself," said Greta.

She got her own coffee. Then she sat in the back booth and looked through the apartment rental ads in the newspaper. Connie brought a carrot muffin for Greta, putting it down with a smile. After about a half an hour Joe came out from the kitchen and sat across from Greta with a plate of pasta covered in meat sauce.

"Connie! Coffee please!" he hollered.

Joe mumbled between mouthfuls of pasta.

"It's your day off?" he asked.

"Yes," said Greta. "I wanted to see if there was any chance you could give me more hours?"

"You want to work more?" asked Joe. "I thought you had another job."

"They cut back my hours," explained Greta. "So I can work as much as you need me now. Except for Sunday."

"I will look at the schedule," said Joe. "Come by tomorrow, I think I can use you on other days when we are busy."

"Oh, that would be so great," Greta said with a big smile.

Joe smiled back warmly with a forkful of pasta in hand and sauce on his lips. Greta left, not before placing her used cup and saucer in the bin for the kitchen staff. Connie smiled and winked at Greta as she poured coffee at one of her tables.

"Have a good one hon," said Connie.

"Thanks Connie, I'll try," Greta replied.

When she arrived at Jeans N Tops there was a young blonde female talking to Jenna at the cash counter.

"Hi Greta," said Jenna. "When you go to the back can you tell Harbinder that Tawny is here for her interview please."

"No problem," Greta said, strutting past, knowing he was looking for her replacement.

She hung up her bag and jacket, changed shoes, touched up her lipstick and then knocked on his office door.

"Come in," said Harbinder.

She opened the door.

"Someone's here for an interview," she said.

"Send her back," he said. "Oh. Here's your wages."

He passed her an envelope with her name on it. Greta took it and went out and told Tawny to go to the office. Knowing that he was always watching them, Greta and Jenna whispered while they worked.

About thirty minutes later, Harbinder came out of the back with Tawny following him like a submissive puppy.

Completely ignoring Greta, he said, "Jenna, this is Tawny."

Tawny offered an eager toothy smile.

"Pleased to meet you Jenna," she said.

Jenna said nothing with a half smile.

"Jenna, can you please show Tawny around the sales floor a little bit?" asked Harbinder. "She'll be starting tomorrow morning."

"Sure, no problem," said Jenna. "Come on. We can start over here."

Jenna led the new hire to the front of the store. She spent about half an hour with Tawny before wrapping it up.

"See you in the morning," Tawny chirped.

Greta and Jenna rolled their eyes at each other. Greta learned what Jenna already knew. This was Harbinder's modus operandi.

That night, when Greta got to her apartment, she opened her pay envelope to find that Harbinder had deducted the staff price for the jeans he gave her from her wages. She filled a short glass with warm wine and sat in a lonely depression thinking about being poor. Her hope was that Joe would give her some busy shifts where she'd make tips.

There was not much wine left, so she opened the mickey of vodka and mixed some with water and orange juice crystals. She brought a kitchen stool into the bathroom and sat in front of the mirror, smoking a cigarette. She used a brush to gently take out some of the teasing in her hair and recurled the top pieces. She applied more rouge and eyebrow pencil.

Then she looked for something to wear. A short black mini skirt, skin tone nylons, her fuchsia camisole, and a black bolero with silver threads would do. A pair of long silver dangly earrings put it over the top. She was ready to traipse up to McCluskey's jazz scene, not before polishing off the rest of the wine and the vodka with orange crystals.

Greta's situation was pretty grim. A half months' rent overdue, she was pregnant and preparing for an abortion. She missed her best friends back home, especially Jeff, but Brenda and Mark too. She began to miss her parents, her aunt Esther, and even Jesse. She felt like a failure and an embarrassment. She didn't see beauty in the mirror anymore and hid behind her makeup, hair, and clothes. She avoided the reality of her life by drinking to forget.

She got soused at McCluskey's, letting men come up to her and buy her one drink after another. She would talk to one man and then walk away to flirt with another. The jazz band was hypnotic and Greta found herself standing amongst people she didn't know that were passing around reefers. She eventually staggered home alone and passed out fully clothed on her bed.

Greta woke with a splitting headache and stumbled to the washroom to throw up in the toilet. As she was plugging in the kettle to boil water for instant coffee she saw that the loveseat was not in front of the door. In her stupor the night before, she must have forgotten to move it.

The door was not locked! She'd been reckless. She quickly locked it and moved the loveseat back. The kettle whistled and she made her coffee, lit a cigarette, and started taking off the clothes she had slept in.

She wasn't wearing her nylons. Her shoes were on the floor at the end of the bed and she was wearing everything else she had on the night before. She didn't see her nylons anywhere. For all she knew, she may have removed them in the restroom at McCluskey's.

The coffee tamed her headache as she removed her crusty mascara with baby oil soaked cotton balls. Squinting, she stepped into the shower and squeezed some shampoo into the palm of her hand. As she lathered her hair, the suds flowed down her neck and down her breasts. She noticed that they were fuller because of the pregnancy. As the lather flowed over them she looked down and felt their size with her hands causing her nipples to become erect. As she moved her hands over her body, she felt her ribcage. Her stomach was still flat. She imagined a seed not bigger than a kidney bean inside her uterus as she moved her hand down between her legs. The warm, soapy water lathered into her pubis as she felt her nubby clitoris. She rinsed off completely and stepped out of the shower onto a towel.

Then she reached for the baby oil bottle that was sitting on the bathroom vanity and poured a generous amount into the palm of her wet hand. Starting at her chest she let the oil flow down her concave stomach, into her belly button, and into her hairy pubis. She spread a towel on the bed, stretched out on her back and with bent knees placed one hand on her left breast and the other between her legs. Twisting one nipple and then the other while she rubbed her oiled clitoris, Greta brought herself to climax and laid there until the rush of oxytocin subsided.

While still naked, she did Jane Fonda's workout to radio music. After which she did her hair and makeup while smoking and drinking coffee. Greta put on plain jeans and a t-shirt, with a jean jacket and sneakers, and started walking over to Joe's.

It was late Saturday morning and the coffee house was bustling. Most tables were full, there were a few spots open at the counter and Connie and Darlene were hustling coffee and breakfast with proficiency. The atmosphere was cheerful with lots of chatter and clinking of dishes and cutlery. Joe's voice could be heard above all others, calling out orders to his kitchen staff. Greta found an unencumbered path to the rear booth where she opened the newspaper while simultaneously watching the activity in the restaurant.

"Just help yourself if you want something Greta. We are slammed," Darlene said as she walked by briskly.

"No prob," said Greta as she spied a moment that wasn't too busy behind the counter.

She got a coffee and sat back down. It was at least thirty minutes or more before there was a lull in activity. Joe came and sat beside Greta so both of their backs were to the wall.

"We are very busy. You want to work today?" he asked.

"Wow," Greta replied. "Yes. But I didn't bring my uniform."

"Find one in the back you can wear," said Joe. "There's extras."

"Ok," said Greta. "I can start right away."

"We will talk about your hours later," said Joe. "I gotta get back in the kitchen."

"Sure, that's fine," said Greta.

Greta was so happy to be done with Jeans N Tops and planned to never show her face there again. She got changed into a uniform that fit her well in the bust but was loose on the bottom. She sinched the apron enough to define her figure and joined Darlene and Connie on the floor.

"Thank God you can help us today," Darlene said as she grabbed two plates off the service window ledge.

Connie came by with an empty coffee pot and said, "Can you work behind the counter? Keep the coffee going and cash people out when they are done?"

"No problem," Greta said with a confident, positive attitude.

She was so happy to be a part of the energy in the room and worked as a team player serving customers at the counter and assisting Darlene and Connie in every way she could. Connie left at six-thirty and Greta and Darlene worked until closing time. It wasn't until the closed sign had been turned and the door was locked from the inside that Joe had time to sit at his booth. He called for Darlene to bring him a coffee. He pulled out a mickey of whiskey and poured a little into his coffee cup.

"Greta, come here!" he hollered, still not hoarse from yelling in the kitchen all day.

Greta stopped what she was doing and joined Joe, sitting across from him at his booth.

" Eat something," he commanded.

"Is there any soup left?" she asked Joe.

"Yes, but not much," he replied. "Go tell the boys you want a bowl of soup."

Greta got up and went to the service window and asked Derek for a bowl of vegetable soup.

"Sure thing Greta," said Derek as he grabbed a bowl and filled it with a ladle from a large pot.

He placed it on the ledge and Greta thanked him.

"I'll sweep as soon as I'm done this soup," she said to Darlene.

Darlene nodded and smiled as she wiped down the counters with a bleach rag.

Greta grabbed a spoon from the utensil tray behind the counter and went and sat back down across from Joe.

"So, you want to work more?" he asked for confirmation.

"Yes. I do," said Greta as she took a spoonful of homemade soup.

"You are a good worker. I can give you full-time," he replied.

"Really? That would be so great!" she exclaimed with delight.

Joe counted as he sipped his coffee and Greta ate her soup. When she was finished, she got up and asked if he wanted anything else.

"No! Be here at two o'clock on Tuesday. You will work Tuesday to Saturday from two until closing," he said, resuming his gruff tone.

"Thank you so much," Greta beamed.

Joe merely glanced at her without lifting his head and carried on counting.

When they were finished cleaning up, Darlene and Greta left and locked the front door. The kitchen staff stayed late to mop and get the kitchen ready for the next day.

When Greta returned to her apartment there were no signs of entry but she went through her precautionary steps relieved that there were no surprises awaiting her. After removing her makeup and gently brushing her hair, she brushed her teeth. Knowing she had a steady full time job gave her some newfound hope.

She remembered the blank cheque in her purse and the traced signatures of her former boss. How could she use it without getting caught and did she even care if she got caught? Maybe if she filled in a figure that looked similar to some of the purchase orders the business had made, it would slip under the radar without detection. For now, she tucked it under her pillow.

She laid back on the bed thinking about the landlord who lived above her and fell asleep with scissors in her hand.

Chapter 14
The Downtown Motel

Her alarm went off at ten. The banks were all closed on Sunday so she wouldn't be able to do anything with the blank cheque yet. Her mission that day was to get through her first modelling job.

She focused on hiding the bald patch on her head. There were only sparse bits of regrowth so far. She took a soft, subdued approach to her makeup, not wanting to look unnatural.

In her mind, she'd decided to pose undraped. It was twice the money and she needed it. After all, she didn't know anybody in the class except for Martin.

She didn't want to have lines on her skin, so she wore a dress and tights with no bra or underwear. Her skin needed to look smooth and supple. The baby oil from the day before had made it dewy.

Walking through the college she dropped out of reminded her of her failure. It was worse than failing, it was giving up. She hadn't actually failed because she never tried. She felt her mother's disappointment as she walked through the fashion design wing. Student works were on display and she felt regret. She could have created some exquisite designs if she would have stuck it out.

She checked the room numbers as she carried on. There was signage with directions to the art department where she needed to be before one o'clock. Once she found the right room, she poked her head in and saw that there were only a couple of artists there so far. They were setting up their easels. She didn't see Martin.

She found a washroom and meandered the halls looking at student art displays. Some of them were quite good and gave her ideas for poses she might do. Since it was Sunday afternoon, there were very few people in the school. It was quiet. Then she heard the familiar voice of Martin call her name. He approached and offered a welcoming handshake.

"You're right on time," he said.

"Yes," she replied.

"Well it's good to see you," he said. "It's a small group so I hope you'll be comfortable with us."

He invited her into the studio classroom and showed her the dressing closet. He confirmed with her that she would be modelling undraped and paid her cash before they started.

"I know this is your first time, so just do whatever you're comfortable with. Whatever comes naturally," he said encouragingly.

She agreed.

"A lot of models like to focus on the clock on the wall or some other focal point to help them hold their pose. Start with some gestures and switch them every three to five minutes. Then we will take a fifteen minute break. When we come back I'd like you to do a couple of twenty to thirty minute poses if you're comfortable holding them that long," he explained.

"Sure. Ok, I got it," she replied.

"We're ready to start when you are," said Martin.

By now the class had about ten people with their easels and supplies set up. She popped into the tiny dressing closet that had no mirror and only a curtain for privacy. She undressed and hung her clothes on a hook.

When she came out, the atmosphere was surprisingly relaxed. Soft rock played quietly out of a boombox in the corner of the room. She stepped onto the stage, shook out her arms and started thinking about Jane Fonda's workout. Using the movements she knew by heart, Greta leaned to one side, grasped her hands over her head and stretched. She held that position while she watched the clock tick three minutes away.

Her next pose was planned in her head and she switched, holding it for another three minutes. She started counting out the three to five minutes in her head so she wasn't always facing the clock. She avoided looking at the artist's faces and remained focused on the task. It went on like this for a few more poses.

"We'll take a break after this one," said Martin.

Greta took a deep breath and stepped down off of the stage, quickly dressed, and went to the public washroom. After a pee break, she sat alone on one of the benches in the hallway. Fifteen minutes went by rather quickly as she saw the artists returning to the room. Greta returned to the tiny change closet, undressed, and got back on stage. She wasn't quite sure what to do next.

"A twenty minute pose this time please," said Martin.

"Ok," replied Greta as she pulled a chair from the back of the stage to the front. She draped a sheet over it and sat with her legs crossed and her hands folded on her knees.

"Good," said Martin. "Continue to feel free to use any of the props as you wish."

Greta nodded.

Then she stared at the clock but also tried to clear her mind. After twenty minutes passed, Greta released the pose and shook out her limbs. She gently stretched the muscles that had started to tingle and fall asleep. Then she spread the sheet on the stage floor and sat down with one leg straight out and the other crossed over it to the outside of the opposite knee. She hugged her bent knee and dropped her head forward so that her face was hidden. She was very relaxed and forgot about the time.

"Ok, that's great Greta. We'll take another break. Thirty minutes this time," said Martin.

Greta became surprisingly comfortable posing nude. All the exercises she'd done gave her the flexibility to twist and stretch herself into interesting positions, and the requirement to hold each pose allowed her to fall into a trance-like state. There was no feeling of objectification coming from the artists who obviously had an advanced appreciation of human shape and form. They were serious about their work. She was in a place where she felt safe and comfortable to be herself. In fact, she had been encouraged to be herself for perhaps the first time in her life.

When the session was complete, Greta got dressed and approached Martin.

"We'll see you next Sunday at the same time?" he queried.

"Yes," answered Greta. "I just wanted to let you know that I quit Jeans N Tops and am full-time at Joe's now."

"Ok, thanks for letting me know," said Martin. "Do you have a way home?"

"I'm going to walk," said Greta.

"Ok," replied Martin. "But if you ever need a lift, that can be arranged. Just let us know."

"Thanks, that's good to know," said Greta.

And she left.

In three hours she had made more money than she would have working at Jeans N Tops for three days. She thought about the blank cheque she was carrying in her purse.

On her way back to the apartment, Greta picked up a bottle of cheap red wine and a two liter bottle of wine cooler. When she got back to the apartment, she grabbed the two uniforms that needed to be washed for her first full-time week ahead. She stuffed them and the rest of her laundry into a garbage bag and changed into a clean pair of tights and a short knit dress. She took the empty mickey from under the kitchen sink and filled it with wine. Then she grabbed a fistful of coins. Off she went to the laundromat feeling in good spirits.

There were a couple of other people in the laundromat including the lady who she had chatted with before. It was the first time washing her new jeans so she put them in with darks because she didn't want to risk ruining her uniforms if they bled. Everything else went in with her uniforms. She discreetly took a gulp of wine from the mickey and dialed Jeff from the payphone. This time she made it a collect call. His mother accepted the charges and gave the phone to him. Greta was very chatty and told him she'd quit the jeans store and was now full-time at Joe's, leaving out the details about Harbinder.

"That's terrific!" exclaimed Jeff encouragingly. "Sounds like Connie and Darlene are great gals to work with."

"Oh my God," said Greta. "They are the best! And they have taught me so much."

"So my friend is going to visit some family for a few days and can give me a ride down Thursday," said Jeff. "If that's alright with you."

"It'd be so great to see you," said Greta. "It's been months. You can do whatever you want while I'm at work. But when I'm off, I'm all yours."

"Awesome," said Jeff. "I can't wait to see you and the Big City."

"I can't wait to see you too," she replied as she took another swig of wine and lit a cigarette.

"My place is really small, but you're welcome to crash with me if you want," she said.

"Whatever works for you. If you're ok with it," said Jeff.

"Of course I am," Greta reassured him. "I can't wait to see you!"

They talked a bit about Brenda and Mark. Brenda was due in three months and Mark was working at the factory. As Greta sipped her wine she thought about her impending appointment at the abortion clinic. She couldn't imagine having a baby and she hated the fact she was pregnant. She had stopped listening to Jeff.

"Maybe we could go to a movie one night?" he asked for the third time.

She snapped out of it and replied, "Oh. Yeah. That'd be swell. I think the new Stallone movie is out. And An Officer And A Gentleman too. I can check the papers."

"Would love to see Rambo," said Jeff. "But whatever you want."

"I'd better go check on my laundry," said Greta.

"Ok," said Jeff. "Good night hon."

"Bye," said Greta. "See you soon."

She hung up and wondered why he had called her hon.

Another mouthful of wine dispelled her musings as she went to transfer her clothes from the washers to dryers. The lady who she had chatted with before was adding liquid fabric softener to a load beside Greta.

"Fancy meeting you here again," she said.

Greta replied, "I'm here at least once a week."

"More than that for me. I do laundry for one of my clients," the lady said.

"Oh really? You do someone else's laundry?" Greta asked.

"Yeah I clean a couple of houses, and one of the old guys gets me to do his laundry too," the lady answered.

"Oh, I see," said Greta. "Keeps you busy then."

"Oh yes," said the lady. "It's worth it. He pays me well, the machines here are nice and big and it gets me out for a while."

"Makes sense," replied Greta. "I guess it's a change of scenery."

"You know, I have a little apartment a couple of blocks down," said the lady. "You can call me anytime. I have an answering machine. Maybe you'd like to come for coffee sometime as a change of scenery for you too."

"Oh that's sweet of you," said Greta. "I don't even know your name."

"Eunice," said the lady.

"I'm Greta," she replied with an outstretched hand.

They shook and Eunice tore a piece of cardboard from a laundry detergent box. She found a pen in her bag and jotted down her name, address, and phone number.

"It's just two blocks down that way," said Eunice, pointing towards the back of the laundromat.

"Thanks a lot," said Greta. "I'm working full-time so I don't know when I'll be able to call you. Maybe on my day off."

"No problem," said Eunice. "Just thought you might like a friend. 'cause I gather you're not from around here."

"You're right," Greta replied. "I'm from up North. Rivertown."

They didn't talk a whole lot after that. But Eunice kept her eye on Greta as she looked through magazines. Greta went to the washroom to hide her drinking from Eunice after that.

When she got home, she drank the rest of the wine and vodka while listening to music and unbagging her clean clothes.

She passed out drunk and woke with a hangover, staggering to the bathroom to throw up. She needed the day to recover, tossing, turning, and moaning between head and stomach pains. She finally fell asleep for several more hours and woke up dehydrated. A long hot bath and several glasses of water put her back to sleep until Tuesday.

Tuesday, Wednesday, and Thursday were routine shifts at Joe's Coffee House. She made a lot of tips and solidified her working relationships with Connie and Darlene. She was encouraged that she had almost enough for the rest of the month's rent because she hadn't found another place to live yet. Everything was either shared bathroom and kitchen, too expensive, or too far from Joe's. It was essential that she stay within walking distance to work.

That night, on her way home, Greta meowed back at the cats in the catwalk and talked to them. A couple of them had gotten friendly with her and approached her and rubbed up on her legs. She had become comfortable and familiar with the neighborhood on her walks to and from Joe's. As she neared her apartment, she pulled out the scissors from her purse. She clutched them in her left hand with the points up towards her forearm, concealed but ready to thrust if she raised her arm. Her key was in her right hand and could also be used as a weapon.

She walked quietly, hypervigilant to every sound, and cognizant that Charlie could be wearing soft soled shoes and hiding in the shadows. There were a few clouds in the evening sky and the moon went into hiding behind one of them as Greta inserted the key into her door. As she pulled out the key, a low monotone voice from behind made her freeze.

"Do you have the rest of your rent money Greta?" Charlie asked.

Greta's heart fell into her stomach. If only she had made out the blank cheque and cashed it. She wasted that beginning of her week recovering from her hangover and hadn't made it to the bank. Now she didn't have all the money for her rent. As she turned around she could barely see Charlie's tall looming silhouette against the blackness of the night. He stood there with his hands in his pockets. Greta gasped.

"I can have it for you tomorrow. I just haven't had time to go to the bank," she said.

She tensed up the grip on her scissors.

Charlie said, "I'm tired of waiting."

He pulled his right hand out of his pocket, stepped towards her, and placed it on her shoulder. He started pushing her into the apartment. She lifted her left hand and thrust the scissors aimlessly at him. She gashed his arm. He was so tall and overpowering.

"You bitch!" he hollered.

Then he hit Greta's arm so hard that the scissors flew across the room. He held her by the arm, twisting it painfully as he pulled her missing nylons out of his right trench coat pocket.

"Stop! You're hurting me!" Greta yelled.

"Shut up, you little tramp," Charlie ordered her as he kicked the door shut.

He squeezed her right arm until the key fell to the floor, turning Charlie's anger to fury. He hit her hard across the face and she fell to the floor. She crawled towards the scissors. As she reached for them, her head was pulled back by her hair. He wrapped Greta's nylons around her neck and kicked the scissors out of reach. He picked her up by the waist and flung her to the bed like a rag doll. She remembered the time her father pushed her mother onto the bed and raised his fist as she screamed.

Greta screamed, "Help!"

He slipped the nylons off her neck, balled them up, and shoved them in her mouth. She managed one final hopeless plea.

"Stop! Please stop," she cried.

There was a loud crash at the door as it busted open with a boot kick.

"What the fuck are you doing?!" a male voice shouted.

Jeff bounded at Charlie and laid his hardest punch across the side of his head knocking him off balance. He nailed him with a second hard blow to the face.

"You fucking bastard!" yelled Charlie.

Greta gagged as she pulled the nylons out of her mouth.

"Oh my God. Jeff. It's you!" she cried.

She ran for the scissors and curled up in the corner with them shaking in her hand. Charlie scrambled out the door as Jeff attended to Greta. He knelt beside her, lowered the scissors and took her in his arms.

"Who the hell was that guy?" he asked.

With a quivering voice she replied, "That's my landlord and I'm late with the rent."

"Jesus Christ," said Jeff. "We gotta get you outta here."

"I tried," said Greta. "I can't afford to move."

"Come on," he said, helping Greta to her feet. "We'll figure something out."

There were bruises starting on Greta's face and neck.

"Maybe we should call the police," Jeff said.

"That won't help," said Greta. "I still owe him rent money and have no place else to go. It'll just make matters worse."

"Where's the nearest payphone?" he asked.

"Through the alley. At the corner by McCluskey's," she said.

"Ok. But you're coming with me," said Jeff. "You're not safe. He could come back."

"Where are we going?" asked Greta in a state of shock.

"Listen, there's gotta be a motel around where you can stay temporarily," said Jeff, shaking her by the shoulders. "We'll look in the phone book."

"Oh. Ok," Greta replied. "Let me check my face in the bathroom first. How's my makeup?"

"Don't worry about that," said Jeff, giving her a hug for reassurance.

"I'm so glad you are here," she wept. "Is it bad?"

"I'm glad I'm here too," said Jeff. "And you are beautiful as always."

Jeff put his arm around Greta's shoulder as any good friend would and they walked through the catwalk under the moon, now out from behind the clouds.

"It's this way," said Greta pointing to the left as they came out the other end of the catwalk.

As they got closer to McCluskey's, Greta pointed out the sign.

"It's in front of that bar, on the corner," she said.

She didn't want to use that payphone because of its location in front of the bar.

The closer they got, the more they could hear music pumping. It had to be close to closing time. There were a few groups standing outside smoking joints in the shadows. As they got closer they could smell it. There was laughing and coughing.

"Hey Greta," they heard.

Greta stopped and turned to see Cory and Graham puffing on a fatty.

"What's up?" Cory asked.

"Oh not much. Just gotta use the payphone," Greta said.

She didn't want them to see her bruised face.

Cory asked, "You wanna join us after?"

Greta said, "Uh no thanks. My friend and I have plans."

"Ok then. See you at Joe's," Cory replied.

"Ok. See ya," said Greta as she walked to the payphone with Jeff.

"Sorry about that," she said to Jeff.

"No problem," he replied.

He reached for the phone book and flipped to the yellow pages.

"Is this one nearby?" he asked Greta as he pointed at an ad.

"I'm not sure. Wanna try it?" she replied.

"Ok, I'll ask their rates and if they are close to here," he said.

They didn't have a pen or paper to write it down. But the cheapest and closest became obvious. From where they were it was past Joe's and walking distance to work.

"We'll ask them to hold a room for us for a couple of hours. That'll give us enough time to get your things together and get there by cab," said Jeff.

"Should we call the cab now too?" asked Greta.

"Yes. We can ask them to be at the apartment in two hours," said Jeff.

"Ok," said Greta. "It sounds like my only option. I can't stay at the apartment. Charlie has gone crazy."

"You're right," said Jeff. "That guy is fucking scary and dangerous."

Jeff made the calls to hold the motel room and reserve the cab. On the walk back, Greta told Jeff that she suspected Charlie had been entering her apartment before, when she wasn't there. She didn't tell him about the rape.

They hurried back to the apartment and gathered up all of Greta's clothes. All of her belongings fit into a suitcase, a duffle bag, her oversized purse, her backpack and a garbage bag. They took another look around to make sure they didn't forget anything.

"Under the sink," said Greta. "There's a container with a lot of change. Could you grab that please?"

"Holy shit this is heavy," Jeff remarked.
"Tips," Greta said.

She picked up the scissors that had nicked Charlie's forearm. There was blood on them. She put them in her purse and left the key on the counter. She even took what was left of the toilet paper. Then they waited with the apartment door wide open in silence, for the taxi as they smoked cigarettes.

They saw the moving lights and heard the tires of the cab pulling into the driveway. Jeff grabbed the heavy suitcase, duffle bag, and the jar of coins. Greta got everything else.

"Come on, let's go," said Jeff.

They hurriedly carried everything up the stairs to the taxi. The driver complied when Jeff asked him to pop the trunk.

"Where do you think you're going?" came a shout from the front of the house.

It was Charlie. He heard the taxi pull up from his main floor residence. He had bandaged his forearm and was still fuming. He approached Greta as she was putting the garbage bag into the back seat.

"You owe me, bitch! I want my money!" he yelled.

Jeff pushed him away from Greta with the full force of his hands on Charlie's chest.

"Get away from her!" he yelled.

"I'm outta here you prick!" yelled Greta as she got into the back seat of the cab.

"Hey man," said the cab driver. "I don't need no drama."

Jeff told Charlie to back off and got into the front seat of the cab.

"Lock your door. Let's get outta here fast," he said.

As the driver started backing up, Charlie banged his fists on the hood of the cab as it pulled out of the driveway. The driver blared the horn several times. Charlie stood on the front lawn of the house watching them with an evil stare. He got smaller and smaller as they drove away.

"Ok now. Where to folks?" asked the cabby with a sigh.

"The Downtown Motel," said Greta.

"No problem," said the cabby. "It's not too far; fifteen minutes max."

"Thanks," said Greta, breathing a sigh of relief.

"Mind if I smoke?" she asked the cabby as she rolled the window down a couple of inches.

"No problem," he replied as he pulled out a cigarette too.

Eventually, they stopped in front of the Downtown Motel. "Here it is," said the cabby.

He opened the trunk and helped Jeff pull the contents out onto the sidewalk. They shook hands and Jeff paid the fare.

"Thanks," said the cabby. "And good luck man. Hope ya ain't stepping outta the frying pan into the fire."

The small lobby of the motel was furnished with an old couch, two matching wooden chairs, a coffee table, and overflowing waste baskets. There were magazines and newspapers strewn about, a couple of large dirty ashtrays, and a well-used coffee station against one wall. There was a payphone in the corner and one vending machine with assorted cold drinks and another with assorted bars, chips, and snacks.

Jeff approached the reception counter. Greta stood beside him with her head down. A slovenly rotund man in a rolling office chair sat with his back to them behind a desk a couple of meters away. He paid no attention to them while he jammed a donut into his mouth and lifted a coffee cup to his lips.

Rather than ring the bell on the counter, Jeff cleared his throat.

The man grunted, "Yeah. Yeah."

He gulped and added, "I'm coming."

Slowly he rolled the chair back and stood up. He hobbled over to the counter with a cigarette butt in his hand. He took a last drag that burnt it down to the filter before extinguishing it in a full ashtray beside the cash register.

"How can I help you?" asked the man.

"We called a couple of hours ago for a room," said Jeff.

"For the both of you?" asked the clerk.

"Well, it's for me," Greta answered.

"But my friend is staying for a couple of days," she pointed to Jeff.

"Oh yes. I remember the call," said the clerk. "How long are you planning on staying?"

"I'm not sure," Greta replied. "Can I pay for one week?"

The clerk explained that Greta could pay one week at a time in advance and that there was a room on the second floor he could give her that faced the street. She gave him cash and he gave her the key.

"The stairs are through that door," said the clerk.

Just relieved to have made it to the room, they laid on the bed and held each other. They left Greta's bags strewn across the floor and fell asleep in embrace.

In the morning, they woke up still in each other's arms and Greta began to cry as she realized where she was, what had happened, and who she was with.

"What's the matter?" asked Jeff as he cradled her head. "He can't hurt you now."

"It's not that," said Greta. "I'm pregnant."

Jeff sat up.

"What?" he asked.

Greta repeated, "I'm pregnant."

Jeff stood up.

"Who's the father?" he asked.

Greta answered, "I don't know."

Jeff began to pace back and forth.

"What do you mean you don't know? How could you not know?" he asked.

"It doesn't matter anyway. I'm getting an abortion," she replied.

Jeff sat back down beside her.

"Greta, don't do something you'll regret," he said.

"I already regret everything. Coming here. Going to school. Quitting school. My life is a mess!" she insisted.

"Honey, things will get better," responded Jeff. "You're just going through a rough patch."

"There were two guys," said Greta. "They were one night stands and I'm not sure which one got me pregnant. I'll never see them again anyway."

"I understand. Things happen when you're partying," he said. "We all make mistakes. But it's not the baby's fault."

"I already have an appointment," she said. "I can't have a baby in a place like this. Plus, I don't have time for a baby. I've thought this through and I'm getting an abortion."

"Look honey," said Jeff as he took her hand. "I've always loved you and we can raise this baby together."

"What?" she asked. "You can't be serious."

"Of course I am Greta. I would do anything for you," he pleaded. "You must know that by now."

She covered her face with her hands and began to cry again.

"But how?" she asked.

"We can work out the details after," said Jeff. "You can come back home and we can get a place together. My job is steady and after the baby is born, you can take some time off."

"Oh my God, Jeff. I can't believe you'd do that," said Greta.

"The baby needs a father," he said as he placed his hand on Greta's stomach.

She wrapped her arms around him.

"You don't have to do this. It's not your responsibility," she said.

"I want to do it. The baby will never know," he said.

They swayed gently side to side hugging as her tears subsided. He gently stroked her back.

"Don't worry. I'll always be here for you, and the baby," he said.

"You must be famished," he said.

"Well not really, but I'm sure *you* could eat," Greta replied.

"There must be someplace around here where I can get us some breakfast," he said.

"I'll get in the shower," she said. "I still have to work today."

"Are you sure? Maybe you should take the day off?" he asked.

"No. I'm sure," replied Greta. "I need to stick with my routine and I couldn't do that to Joe and Connie and Darlene."

"Ok, I'll ask the front desk where I could get some breakfast for us," said Jeff.

"Take the key," she replied.

"Alright. I'll be back in a flash," he said as he left.

She opened her suitcase and unzipped her duffle to find one of her uniforms. She placed it on a hanger on the shower curtain rod so the steam would release the wrinkles. She removed her toiletries, makeup, blow dryer, and curling iron from her backpack and placed them on the tiny vanity.

Everything in the room was old, worn, and dingy. Greta opened the dusty old curtains to a window that hadn't been cleaned in months, or years. She cranked the window open to let some of the stale, musty air escape. She looked down at the street below. It wasn't the pretty part of town but she was away from her rapist.

The shower was steaming as Greta got in. There was black mold in the corners so she tried to avoid touching anything disgusting. She washed as quickly as she could and toweled off in one place before stepping out onto an old bathmat. She slid into her flip flops and put on underwear and a camisole.

Then she went over to the open window again for some fresh air. Jeff was returning with a styrofoam take-out container and a paper bag. Her heart warmed for her friend who wanted to be her partner in life and create a family. She'd known him for years but grappled with stepping into the domain of lovers with him. In a couple of minutes he came through the door bringing hot food and coffee.

"Oh my God," said Greta. "Is that coffee I smell!?"

"Yup," answered Jeff. "I got you a large one with cream, sugar, and sweetener on the side."

"Sweet," she said.

"Me or the coffee?" Jeff asked.

"Both," said Greta as she reached for the sweetener and a creamer. "You know me so well."

"I got scrambled eggs, a double order of home fries, bacon, and toast," said Jeff.

There was peanut butter and jam on the side and two forks.

"You go ahead and start," said Greta. "I'm going to drink this coffee and dry my hair."

"How was the shower?" asked Jeff as he chomped on a piece of bacon.

"Disgusting!" Greta declared. "I'll pick up some Comet. You can still shower, just don't touch the gross stuff."

"Ok. Eew. Good to know," said Jeff as he continued to eat.

Greta dried her hair upside down and pinned a longer section over the thin spot. She didn't want Jeff to see it and ask questions.

"Come and join me while it's still half warm," said Jeff.

"Coming," said Greta.

She pulled a chair up to the tiny wobbly wooden table. She took a piece of toast and opened a peanut butter.

"I'm not really hungry, but this is good. Thanks so much for getting it for us," she said.

"I was starving," said Jeff. "Eat some potatoes, there's lots."

Greta stuck a piece of potato with her fork and dipped it in ketchup.

"Mmm," she said. "Where'd you get this? It's almost as good as Joe's."

"There's a diner up the street called Fat Al's," answered Jeff.

"That's handy," said Greta.

"Oh, and the day shift lady downstairs is Marge. She said you can get coffee in the lobby anytime too," he added.

"I hope she will lend me the vacuum cleaner," said Greta. "This place is pretty dusty."

"Well it ain't no palace, but it'll be ok for now," he said. "And as long as you're here, it's got a princess."

They smiled softly at each other. Greta gathered strength from Jeff's words, but still wasn't sure how things could work in reality.

After a prolonged silence Greta said, "I'd better get ready for work. I need to cover up these bruises."

"You look beautiful no matter what and I'm sure you can work some magic on that," he said encouragingly.

"I think I might even have a kerchief I can tie around my neck," said Greta.

"What will you do while I'm at work?" she asked him.

"Oh I don't know," said Jeff. "I'll find something to do. Maybe I'll go for a long walk or read a book."

They both laughed a little because Jeff was known for enjoying long walks and occasionally getting lost in a good book for hours. He walked her to work and they entered Joe's Coffee House together where she introduced him to Connie.

"Connie. This is my friend Jeff from back home," she told her.

"Hello. Pleased to meet you," she said, extending her free hand.

She held an empty coffee pot in the other.

"The pleasure is all mine," said Jeff as they shook. "Nice place."

"Thanks dear," Connie replied. "Feel free to stick around for a coffee. We have some amazing fresh apple pie too."

"It really is the best," Greta affirmed. "Better than my mom's even. Sit down and I'll get you a piece."

He stayed for a piece of scrumptious pie and a cup of coffee. When he tried to pay, Connie said, "Nonsense! Just come and get the fair lady at closing time."

"I promise. I will," Jeff replied with a warm smile.

After he left, Connie said, "Wow, he's sweet. And handsome. Did he give you that hickey?"

Realizing her scarf had twisted to expose part of her bruised neck, Greta blushed.

"Oh my God. Yes," she lied. "We got a little carried away last night."

There was a mirrored portion of the wall behind the back bar that Greta used to adjust her scarf as she gathered her composure and went back to her customers. Whenever she went to the washroom she checked her makeup. Her concealer and compact were in her apron pocket so she could touch up as needed. The buildup of cosmetics was beginning to look thick.

Connie left an hour after Darlene arrived for the evening shift. Each time the bells on the door chimed, the women glanced up from whatever they were doing to see who was coming and going. It was Cory and Graham.

"Your friends are here," Darlene said with a wink.

Greta went through the motions and fake pleasantries as she brought Cory and Graham their coffees. They got the usual, including dessert at the end of their meal. Cory was flirtatious and inquisitive about who Greta was with the night before, at the payphone in front of McCluskey's.

"Who was that guy you were with last night?" he asked.

"One of my friends from back home," said Greta. "He's just visiting."

"Oh, you should've introduced him to us and come in for a beer," said Graham.

"I know," said Greta. "But we had other plans. Catching up you know."

Greta took their empty dessert dishes away, refreshed their coffees and began to walk away just as the door chimes rang.

Without turning around she said, "The kitchen is closed."

"That's ok," said the familiar voice. "Just a coffee will do."

Greta turned to see Jeff's smiling face. He was shaved, showered, and wearing new clothes. She approached to greet him.

"You look great," she said brightly.

He took a seat at the counter as Darlene poured him a cup.

"Thanks," he said. "How was your shift?"

"Anytime doll," said Darlene. "Always a good shift working with this gal."

"I just have to cash out my last customers and clean up. I should be done in about half an hour," said Greta.

"No rush," said Jeff. "I've got no place else to be, or where I'd rather be."

The first chance Darlene got, she whispered to Greta, "Oh my God. He is adorable."

Cory walked up to the cash.

He opened his wallet and asked, "What do I owe you dear?"

Greta handed him his cheque.

"Cory, Graham, this is my friend Jeff from back home," she said.

"Hey, pleased to meet you," said Jeff standing up and extending his hand.

Cory and Graham were slightly taller and bigger than Jeff. But Jeff was very confident and possessed a wholesome uncontrived masculinity.

"So, you came down just to see Greta?" asked Cory.

"Can you think of a better reason to be here?" Jeff quipped.

"The food I guess," said Cory. "Enjoy your visit."

Cory overtly overtipped Greta before leaving with Graham. Darlene locked the door behind them and turned the closed sign.

"Let's clean up this joint and get outta here," said Darlene.

"You said it!" Greta concurred enthusiastically.

"Is there anything I can do?" asked Jeff.

Darlene and Greta simultaneously said, "No!"

They laughed as Joe came out from the kitchen and took the cash tray out of the register. He sat in his usual booth.

"You got any change girls?" Joe asked in his loud kitchen voice.

"Nope, we already did that Joe," said Darlene as she brought him a coffee.

He pulled a mickey of whiskey out of his pocket and added a drop to his coffee.

"Good girls!" he said.

There was a great spirit of camaraderie in his voice.

After they closed, Jeff and Greta walked back to the Downtown Motel. She was impressed with Jeff. He looked and smelled great.

There were various unusual characters hanging out on the street, including sex trade workers waiting for johns. A dark car with blacked out windows pulled up beside a woman who was very scantily clad. She was standing at the edge of the curb. A man got out and approached her. He grabbed her roughly by the arm. That's when Greta realized it was Daryl.

"Oh my God," she whispered to Jeff, grabbing his arm tightly.

"I know that guy," she said, lowering her head.

They slowed down a bit and walked a cautious distance away from what was going on. Daryl opened the back door of the car and pushed the woman inside.

"You've got a job," he said harshly.

The woman got into the back seat where a man was waiting for her.

Jeff hung onto Greta and softly reassured her, "Don't worry. Just keep walking."

As they walked passed, Daryl caught a glimpse of Greta and gave her an evil glare of recognition. She looked away and started walking faster, tugging on Jeff's sleeve. Jeff looked back at Daryl who was still staring at the two of them. Greta didn't see Daryl point his finger at them, but Jeff did. It looked like he was pointing a gun as he got back into the driver's seat and slowly stalked them.

"Who the hell is that guy?" Jeff asked.

The dark car briefly paused as they scaled the steps of the motel.

"Some guy I met at McCluskey's one night. He didn't handle my rejection very well," Greta simply replied.

"He seriously gives me the creeps," said Jeff.

"Is he the one?" he asked.

"The one what?" asked Greta.

Standing at the front door was a big man who looked like a heavyweight boxer. He opened the door for Greta and Jeff.

"Good evening folks," he said.

"Good evening. Good evening," said Greta and Jeff in tandem.

"You know," Jeff said to Greta.

"God no," she scowled.

A man and woman were talking to the night clerk about getting a room at the reception counter.

The man said, "We don't need the whole night. A couple of hours will do."

"Look. It's by the night. We don't have hourly rates," said the clerk.

"Fine," said the man, slapping his credit card on the counter.

Greta and Jeff pushed the door to the stairwell open and went up to their floor where they saw a man knocking on the door across from Greta's room. The door opened as they approached. There stood a woman wearing a black teddy, fishnet stockings, and knee high patent leather boots. Her black hair was piled high on her head, and she wore excessive makeup with cherry red lips. They expressed a familiarity with one another.

"Peter, you're right on time," she said with a sultry voice.

She grabbed his hand and pulled him into the room roughly, glanced at Greta and Jeff, and closed the door. Greta and Jeff looked at each other wide-eyed and quickly got in their own room.

Greta was amazed when she turned on the light. It smelled like air freshener and bleach and there was a bouquet of flowers on the little wobbly wooden table by the window.

"What did you do?" she asked excitedly.

She was stunned, hung up her jacket and kicked off her shoes. She went into the bathroom. It was spotless. All of the black mold from around the shower was gone. The tile floor, sink and toilet were all pearly white with the strong smell of bleach. There was even a new vinyl shower curtain.

"This is amazing!" she exclaimed.

"I had time, so I went and got some cleaning supplies," said Jeff.

"You are a dream," said Greta. "Did you vacuum?"

"Yes. Marge showed me where the vacuum was and said you could use it any time," answered Jeff. "I used carpet powder first."

"And the flowers," Greta said, as she walked over to the table. There was a bottle of red wine and two plastic cups tucked in behind the flowers.

"The table doesn't wobble anymore," she laughed.

"I know. Do you want a little wine?" he asked as he grabbed the bottle and unscrewed the top.

He poured half a glass for each of them.

"To the prettiest woman in my life," he said.

They sipped and sat down. Greta grabbed the wine bottle and filled her cup. They continued the hard discussion about her pregnancy, with Greta saying it was her choice and she wasn't sure what to do. Jeff tried to convince Greta to keep the baby and let him be the father, reiterating that he would be there for her through anything. She knew he was leaving in two days.

"You've gotta go back to work," said Greta. "And I'm gonna get out of this motel as soon as I can afford a real apartment."

"Come on Greta," he begged. "You know it's not that easy. Otherwise you would have done it by now."

Greta felt discouraged.

"Exactly why I need to get the abortion," she said.

They argued about it and finally decided to try to enjoy the time they had together until Jeff had to go back home.

"As long as you know that I will be here for you if you decide to keep the baby," he said. "Ok?"

"Ok," said Greta. "But how can I go back home? My parents are embarrassed of me."

" Never mind what your parents think. I've got a good job and we can make it if you come back and let me help you," said Jeff. "We'll find our own place and take care of each other."

"I don't want to be a burden to you and make you do this just because you don't want me to get an abortion," said Greta.

"Just promise me you'll think about it. Please," he pleaded.

"I will," she replied.

"Let's get some sleep, it's been a long couple of days," said Jeff.

And he laid back on the bed. She laid beside him but couldn't stop thinking of his conditional promise that he'd be there for her if she decided to keep the baby. She didn't believe he'd be there for her if she didn't keep it. It was awkward, but she fell asleep with her head on his shoulder.

Chapter 15
Stu to The Rescue

Jeff left on Monday afternoon. His absence left Greta feeling vulnerable and confused. Going to work was fine but walking home alone at night was scary now that Daryl had seen her go into the Downtown Motel. There were always one or two women working at the curb near the motel and the woman across the hall from her had men visiting her regularly at night. The doorman Stu trained and worked at a gym during the day and worked some busier nights at the motel to control riffraff.

Greta thought about the promise Jeff had made and was now questioning herself about the abortion. Her appointment was on Friday and she knew if she didn't do it then, the window of opportunity would close. She loved

Jeff as a friend but didn't know if she could spend her life with him just because of a baby he convinced her to keep.

She was getting ready for work on Thursday when there was a knock at the door. It was unusual. No one she knew, knew that she was staying there. It must be Marge, she thought to herself. The knock came again as Greta looked through the peephole. It was the lady from across the hall. Greta opened the door and greeted her neighbor.

She was an attractive woman, not old, but more mature in every way than Greta. She was sexy but rough around the edges. Wrapped in a flannel robe with her artificially black hair piled on her head, she looked like she could have just gotten out of bed after sleeping with her makeup on.

She said, "Sorry to bother you, but is your name Greta?"

Greta replied, "Yes. How did you know?"

"I'm Fran by the way," she said. "A friend of mine was asking about you."

Greta thought one of Fran's clients had seen her and was inquiring for sex.

"You mean," Greta paused and cleared her throat. "One of your male friends?"

Fran chuckled, "No hon. A girlfriend of mine who's seen you walking home at night."

"Oh," Greta blushed. "Why was she asking about me?"

"She asked if you knew Daryl," said Fran.

Greta broke out in a nervous sweat.

"I met him once a the bar," she said. "That's all."

"Well hon," said Fran. "You musta made quite the impression. Because he's asking about you."

"Well why? What does he want?" asked Greta.

"I'll be straight with you hon. He probably wants to make you one of his girls," said Fran. "Around here, he's got a few working for him. It's his territory."

"Oh my God," said Greta. "No offence Fran, but I don't wanna do that. I didn't know you worked for him."

"None taken hon," Fran replied proudly. "I don't work for him. Nobody's my boss. I throw a few bucks Stu's way and no one messes with me. I'm a free agent."

"I've got a job," said Greta. "I'm a waitress."

"Yeah, yeah," said Fran. "I hear ya hon. We all gotta start somewhere. Just watch your back, 'cause he's seen you around."

"Thanks for the heads-up Fran," said Greta as she slowly closed the door.

Greta took the envelope with the traced signatures and blank cheque out of her purse and sat down at the little wooden table by the window. She found a scrap of paper from a magazine that she could practice the forgery on and decided that an amount between three fifty and four hundred would go unnoticed because many of the purchase orders and salaries for Jeans N Tops were in that range. She worked out the signature, then put in her name and the amount of three hundred and eighty-six dollars and thirty-five cents on the cheque.

Before going to work, Greta took the cheque to the bank and acted like she was cashing her regular wages. The bank teller made no remark and asked if she wanted cash or if she wanted to deposit it. Greta asked to have two hundred deposited and to get the rest in cash.

At work that night, Cory and Graham came in around their usual time.

"Hi guys. You're so predictable," she said with a laugh. "Do you want menus? Joe's got a to-die-for rib special today."

Graham said, "You don't need to twist my arm."

"Mashed potato or fries," she asked.

"Gimme the fries please," said Graham.

"Same for me hon," said Cory. "Sounds delish."

He licked his lips flirtatiously.

Greta brought coffee and flirted with them. When it was nearing closing time Cory walked up to the cash register.

Greta said, "Could you wait outside for a sec? There's something I want to talk to you about."

"Sure, no problem hon," he smiled. "Anything for you."

"I'll be right back Darlene. I'm just going to talk to Cory outside for a minute," said Greta.

"Ok," said Darlene as she emptied coffee grounds into the trash. "I'll be right here when ya get back."

Cory and Graham were undoubtedly planning to shoot pool at McCluskey's. When Greta got outside she asked Graham if she could have a moment alone with Cory.

"Yeah. Sure. Whatever," said Graham, as he walked a few feet away from them.

Curious why Greta wanted to talk to him alone he asked, "What's up sugar? Your friend gone back?"

"Yes, he has," answered Greta contritely. "But that's not what I want to talk to you about."

"Well, what is it?" he asked. "You want us to wait for you so you can come with us to McCluskey's?"

"No Cory," Greta said. "It's about that night we spent together."

Cory's eyes widened, "I thought you said everything was fine."

"Well, it's not," she said.

Cory began to fidget and pace while Graham smoked a cigarette a short distance away.

"Fuck," he said. "You mean you're knocked up?!"

"Yes," said Greta. "But I can't be sure it's you."

"What do you mean?" Cory asked with a sense of shock. "You were with someone else?"

"Yes," said Greta. "There was someone else around that time. But don't worry. I'm getting an abortion."

"Oh," Cory sighed. "That's a relief."

"Yeah," said Greta. "I just wanted to let you know."

"Ok, thanks," said Cory.

In a hurry to leave he said, "See you around."

Greta heard him mutter, "Come on Graham. Let's get the hell outta here."

She returned to the diner.

"Everything Ok?" asked Darlene.

"Oh yeah," Greta replied smugly. "Just fine. Perfectly fine."

She found out everything she needed to know from Cory's reaction and resigned herself to the fact that he didn't care.

They finished cleaning and setting up the restaurant for the next day. In the back room, she put her fall trench coat on over her uniform. She and Darlene said good night to Joe. After Darlene locked the front door they went their separate ways.

She was alone again, on her way back to the motel, feeling tense. She slipped her hand into her purse and took out her scissors. She'd cleaned Charlie's blood from them with the leftover bleach Jeff had bought to clean the bathroom. She carried them in a concealed manner tucked in the sleeve of her coat.

Ahead, she could see the woman who had been reeled into Daryl's dark car the night she and Jeff were walking back to the motel. The woman paced back and forth on a small section of the curb. She stopped whenever a car slowed, with her hand on her waist she jutted her hip out. The woman saw Greta distancing herself as she approached.

She called out, "Hey! You!!"

Greta pretended to ignore her and kept walking. From her periphery she could see the woman coming towards her.

"Hey! I said you!!" the woman hollered and approached.

She stepped in front of Greta as a dark car pulled up to the curb. Greta froze.

"My boss wants to talk to you," she said.

The woman grabbed Greta's arm tightly and said, "You're coming with me."

"Get your hands off of me," Greta said as she pulled and broke free.

Daryl quickly got out of the dark car.

"Is this the one?!" the woman yelled.

Daryl declared, "That's her!! Hold her!!"

The woman made another grab at Greta, saying, "You ain't going nowhere honey."

Greta raised the hand with her scissors and stabbed downward onto the woman's arm. She ran.

Daryl yelled, "Get her!"

And the two chased Greta down the sidewalk. Greta had her work sneakers on and could outrun the woman who wore stilettos. Daryl was gaining on her.

In front of the Downtown Motel, Greta turned, faced Daryl and the bleeding woman, thrusting her scissors.

She screamed, "Get away from me!"

Stu bounded out the front door when he saw what was happening. Larger than life, he got in between Greta and her assailants.

"Is there a problem here?" he asked.

He was as big as a tree or the three of them put together. Daryl and the woman backed down and left.

Stu said, "Stay away from them two. They're trouble and they're banned from this establishment for life."

Greta caught her breath and thanked Stu as they walked together into the motel. The night clerk, Dan, was standing behind the counter with a shotgun.

He said, "We don't stand for no trouble around here."

Greta said, "Sorry Dan."

Dan replied, "It ain't your fault hon. Them two is real trouble. You alright?"

"Yup," answered Greta. "I'm fine. Thanks to Stu."

"Ok then," said Dan. "We're here if you need anything."

Greta said good night and thanked Stu and Dan again before going up to her room. With the lights out, she peeked through the curtain in the direction of Daryl's car. He was yelling at the woman. Then he hit her. He left her on the street and drove away in his dark car.

Greta knew they wouldn't give up now that they knew she had no one to protect her when she was walking home at night. Dan and Stu might be able to protect her in the motel, but when she went out to work, she was an open target. The only thing Greta could do was call her mother. She quickly changed out of her uniform and into jeans and a t-shirt. Then she went down to the lobby to use the payphone.

"Hello?" said Myra with the familiar lilt in her voice.

"Collect call from Greta. Will you accept the charges?" asked the operator.

"Mom, it's me," said Greta.

"Greta, is that you? What time is it?" Myra asked.

"Ma'am, will you accept the charges?" the operator repeated.

"Yes," said Myra.

Looking at the wall clock behind the reception counter, Greta said, "It's after eleven."

"It's late," Myra replied. "Why are you calling so late?"

"I know ma. I'm sorry," said Greta. "I wanna come home."

"You called to tell me this now? At this hour?" Myra questioned.

"I can't stay here anymore," said Greta. "I wanna come home."

"Well, I guess you wouldn't be asking unless there was a problem," said Myra. "Did something happen?"

"I couldn't afford the apartment anymore," said Greta. "I didn't know the rent cheque was canceled."

"Well, you've been charging a lot of long-distance calls to me. You didn't expect me to keep paying for everything?" Myra asked rhetorically. "Give me the address where you are."

"It's called the Downtown Motel," she replied.

Greta gave her the address.

Myra said, "I'll talk to your father. But it's late. So call me back in the morning."

"I know I've disappointed you mom. And I've made some stupid choices I regret, but right now I'm in a mess and I need your help," Greta said with a quiver in her voice.

"Ok. Don't worry about it now. We'll talk about it later," said Myra. "Call me in the morning. Ok? The long-distance is getting expensive."

"Ok. Sorry, and thanks ma," Greta replied as a mascara stained tear rolled down her cheek.

Dan and Stu couldn't help but overhear Greta's side of the conversation and watched her with concern.

"You gonna be alright?" asked Dan.

"I don't know," Greta replied. "I'll call my mom back in the morning."

"Well don't worry about a thing down here. Me and Stu got things covered," said Dan.

"Ok. You guys are the best," said Greta.

She went upstairs to her room. She soaked some cotton balls in baby oil and rinsed her face. Then she laid on top of the bed and fell asleep with the bloody scissors in her hand.

Chapter 16
No Choice

When Greta woke, she forgot where she was, thinking back to the apartment. The blood on the scissors had dried while she slept. In the bathroom, she plugged the sink and placed the scissors in there. Then she poured some leftover bleach over them before going to call her mother. She was nervous and afraid of being rejected.

"You have a collect call from Greta," said the operator. "Do you accept the charges?"

It was a reminder of the expense her mother had incurred on her account.

"Yes. I accept," Myra replied.

She was wide awake. Her voice was bright and clear.

"Hello Greta," she said.

"Hi ma," said Greta. "Good morning."

"Is it?" her mother asked.

"No, I guess not," said Greta.

"Your dad left at two," said Myra. "He couldn't sleep after I told him you called."

"Oh my goodness," said Greta. "You mean he's on his way?"

"Yes, we figured he should be there between nine and ten," said Myra.

"Oh mom. Thank God," said Greta. "I'll go pack my stuff now."

"Ok," said Myra. "Be ready."

"I will," her voice cracked.

Myra hung up abruptly. It was already half past eight. Greta quickly told Marge she was leaving. Then she ran upstairs and started hurriedly throwing her things into her assorted bags.

She rinsed and dried the scissors and put them in her purse. While she waited at the window for her father she dreaded the pregnancy that had only been disclosed to Jeff.

There it was! A green Chrysler LeBaron pulled up in front of the motel. She ran downstairs as fast as she could. Her dad was already walking up the front steps. She greeted him as he opened the door to the shabby little lobby.

"Hi dad. You got here so fast," said Greta.

Skipping any formalities he asked, "Where's your stuff?"

"Upstairs, in my room," said Greta.

"Well let's get to it," he replied.

Marge interrupted, "Is this your father?"

Greta said, "Yes. Marge. This is my dad, Sullo. Dad, this is Marge."

"Hello," he said without interest.

"Where's your stuff?" he asked his daughter again.

"Can you say good-bye to the others for me?" she asked Marge.

"Of course," Marge replied. "Run along. Don't keep your dad waiting."

Greta led the way through the doorway, up the stairs to room 208. Just as they were approaching her door, Fran's door opened. A disheveled man, wearing yesterday's crumpled suit, was saying goodbye to Fran. She was wearing a see through black nighty and smoking a cigarette. Both Greta and Sullo averted their eyes as they entered Greta's room.

Once they were behind the closed door of 208, Sullo said, "Well this is the closest thing to hell I've ever seen."

They silently gathered Greta's things and loaded them into the trunk and back seat of the LeBaron. It was late fall and there was a nip in the air. Marge came out carrying two styrofoam cups with lids.

"Coffee to get you going," she said.

"Oh Marge, thank you," said Greta. "Say bye to Dan and Stu for me."

"I will dear," said Marge. "You deserve better than this old rat trap. Go on now. You're daddy's waiting."

He was behind the steering wheel.

"Can you do me a favor?" Greta asked.

"Anything. What is it hon?" she asked.

Greta pulled two pieces of paper out of her jean jacket pocket and handed them to Marge.

"Could you please call these people and tell them I'm sorry I can't come to work?" said Greta.

"Consider it done," said Marge. "Now go on. Get outta here."

Marge held the passenger door for Greta. She got in with a coffee in each hand. Marge slammed the door shut for her as Greta smiled sadly, eyes welling. Marge waved as the car drove away.

"Do you want a coffee dad?" Greta croaked.

"Wait until we get on the highway," her father replied.

She placed one coffee in a cup holder and started sipping the other. The skies were grey and easy on the eyes. Within thirty minutes they were on the highway heading north out of the city.

Sullo said, "I'll take that coffee now."

Greta took the cup from the holder, removed the lid and passed it to her dad.

"It's still warm. But it's got milk and sugar in it," she said.

She knew he always took it black.

"That's ok," said Sullo. "I saw a place where we can gas up and get some breakfast."

"Ok," said Greta.

Sullo drove for a couple of hours before turning into a gas station. He pulled up beside the pumps and rolled down his window as an attendant approached.

"Fill 'er up. Regular," he said to the attendant.

"Yes sir," replied the attendant who noticed the back seat of the car loaded up.

The attendant cleaned the bug splattered windshield of the car while the gas tank was filling. Sullo got out and stretched his legs.

"We're going to get something to eat so I'll pay inside," he told the attendant.

"No problem sir," said the attendant.

Sullo was not too tall, of average height, but was a very husky man with a husky voice, big strong hands, and a ruggedness that showed he was used to a hard day's work. He parked the car in front of the restaurant. They got out and entered.

"I'm just gonna use the washroom first," said Greta.

"Ok," said Sullo. "I'll get a table."

The waitress automatically brought coffee and menus to the table. When Greta got to the table she didn't have much time to look over the menu.

Sullo said, "Trucker's Special, sunny side up with rye toast please."

The waitress turned to Greta and asked, "What'll you have dear?"

"Um… whole wheat toast with peanut butter please," Greta answered. "And more coffee."

Sullo inhaled his meal with gulps of hot black coffee while Greta dipped and nibbled on her toast. The waitress brought the cheque. Sullo looked at it, pulled out his wallet, gave her a twenty.

"Keep the change," he said.

He got up and Greta followed as he paid for the gas. "Wait here," he said. "I'm going to use the toilet."

She could see that the wind had picked up and there was a mist in the air. They had several hours of driving to do and Sullo looked tired. He turned on the wipers as the drizzle turned to rain. The wind got stronger and the rain began to freeze. The further north they got the colder it got. Visibility was poor as Sullo tried to tail a transport truck ahead of them just to stay on the road. It gained speed and soon was out of sight. The freezing rain was accumulating on the windshield and the road conditions had become treacherous.

"We're going to have to pull over," said Sullo as the car swerved.

"Ok dad," said Greta as she clutched the sides of her seat.

She remembered a time when she'd been out fishing with him. The weather turned quickly while they were on the water and they needed to get back to camp fast. The boat bounced on the waves splashing ten feet high. Sullo made sure that Greta's life jacket was secure and he told her to stay low and hold tight. There was a chance they could capsize and end up in the torrent, but her dad navigated the waves head on and got them home safely.

As Sullo began to slow down the car they faintly saw a sign ahead. It was a motor lodge with a flashing red neon vacancy sign.

"I'm beat anyway," said Sullo. "I'll see if they can give us a room to wait out the storm."

Greta was silent.

Sullo pulled up in front of the entrance, left the car running and ran inside. Greta couldn't see through the ice pellet splattered windshield, but her dad came back with a room key. He gave the windows a good scraping then backed the car up slowly and parked in front of the third door from the office. He went ahead and unlocked the door so Greta could run in from the car. It was a clean spartan room with a bathroom, tv, phone, two beds, and small table with two chairs.

"I'm going to take a shower," said Sullo. "You can find something on the tv."

"Ok," said Greta as she picked up the remote control and sat on one of the beds.

Sullo came out of the bathroom wearing his white underwear and undershirt. He turned the heat up in the room. Then he lifted the covers of the bed closest to the door and slid in.

"I'm going to sleep until the storm passes," he said.

"Sure dad," said Greta as she lowered the volume on the tv and got comfortable in the other bed. She felt safe with her dad and eventually fell asleep too.

She was disoriented when she woke. She heard the tv and saw her dad sitting in a chair watching the news. He was fully clothed and wide awake. She got up and went to the washroom.

When she came he asked, "Are you ready to go?"

Greta answered, "Yes."

It was night. The storm had passed and the roads had been plowed and salted. With a full tank of gas, they could make it the rest of the way home. They didn't speak the rest of the way as Greta watched the frozen moonlit fields go by.

The porch light was on when they got home that night. Sullo carried the heavy suitcase and duffle bag while Greta took the rest of her things.

When they entered he said, "Put your things in your room."

"Ok dad," she replied.

"Kiitos," she said, which meant thank you.

And she went downstairs to her old room.

Chapter 17
The Proposal

Greta woke up in her old bed in the house where she grew up. Everything smelled clean and familiar. She got up and went to the washroom where there were fresh towels, new soap, shampoo, a new toothbrush, clean bathrobe and slippers; all neatly arranged for her.

After freshening up with a quick shower in the sauna, Greta went upstairs and there was her mother in the kitchen. Jesse was sitting at the breakfast table.

"Hi ma," said Greta as she opened the cupboard and reached for a coffee cup.

"Hello," said Myra.

The coffee had just finished brewing. As it made its final sputters, Greta pulled it off it's element and poured a brimming cup.

"Mmm," said Greta. "Best coffee ma."

Myra looked over at Greta and smiled.

"Sit down," she told her. "I'm making pancakes."

Myra's pancakes were the best. All of the kids' friends, including Sasha and Brenda, looked forward to them when they slept over. They were thin and fried in butter until they had a crispy lattice edge on them. Myra's mouth-watering pancakes were served with lingonberry preserves and a drizzle of syrup. They were best with a cup of coffee or a glass of cold milk.

Jesse washed down a bite of pancake with milk.

"What are you doing here? I thought you went away to school," she asked pointedly.

Greta replied, "I changed my mind. Good morning to you too."

"Oh, ok," said Jesse. "I was just asking."

She finished her milk, got up from the table, and left the room.

Then Myra asked, "So, how far along are you?"

"What?" asked Greta. "What do you mean?"

"You're pregnant," said Myra.

"How did you know?" asked Greta.

"A mother knows," said Myra. "What else could it be?"

"Well, yes. You're right," Greta affirmed.

"Who's the father?" asked Myra.

"Just some guy I met down there," said Greta. "He doesn't want to be a father."

"Well, if he's the father, he needs to support that child," said Myra.

"I don't even know if I'm keeping it," whispered Greta firmly.

"What do you mean?" asked Myra, raising her voice.

"Ma, I can get an abortion you know," Greta whispered.

"Well," said Myra crossly. "I would never think of such a thing."

"It's my choice," said Greta firmly.

"And it's my choice to allow you to stay under my roof," said Myra.

"Or not," she added harshly.

Just then Sullo walked into the kitchen.

"What's going on? This is my roof by the way," he said.

They both shut up.

Sullo opened the cupboard, grabbed his favorite mug and poured a coffee. His imposing figure overpowered the energy in the room as he took a gulp of the black brew.

"Could you two talk like civilized human beings?" he asked.

Sullo had gotten sober over the past several months and took a personal oath never to touch a drop of alcohol again.

Myra and Greta remained silent.

Sullo asked, "So, what are you arguing about?"

"Greta is pregnant," Myra disclosed.

Greta's skin flushed with shame as she lowered her eyes.

"Ok then," said Sullo. "What's the big deal?"

"What do you mean what's the big deal?" Myra asked angrily.

"Myra, it's just a baby," said Sullo.

"Just a baby! Just a baby!" yelled Myra. "What will the neighbours think? What will the people at church think?"

"Who cares what they think? Only you," he said firmly. "I don't give a damn what they think."

Myra turned beet red and stormed out of the kitchen. She slammed the door to her bedroom.

"She'll get over it," Sullo said to his daughter.

"Thanks dad," Greta said.

She pursed her lips. He touched her shoulder gently before topping up his coffee and going out to the garage.

Greta went to her room and began unpacking.

She dug down to the bottom of her purse to where her scissors had migrated. She held them and thought of the nights she had gotten through with them in her hand. She didn't need them now and put them in the top drawer of the sewing table with the fabric scissors and pinking shears. As she was hanging one of her sweaters there was a light tapping at her door.

"Come in," she said.

Myra opened the door, holding an empty laundry basket.

"You can put your dirty stuff in here," she said as she placed it at the foot of the bed.

"Ok," Greta replied. "I didn't plan for this to happen ma. It was a mistake."

"Your dad is right though," Myra admitted. "We'll figure it out."

"I know this must be hard for you and I'm sorry," said Greta. "I'll leave as soon as I can."

"It's not that," said Myra. "I just want what's best for you."

"I know ma," said Greta. "But I need a chance to try to figure things out for myself."

"Ok," said Myra. "Would you like to come to church with us tomorrow morning?"

"I'll think about it," said Greta.

After she sorted and put away most of her things she used the downstairs phone to call Jeff.

"Hi, it's me," she said when he answered.

There was no long-distance operator to go through.

"Greta, I'm so glad you called," he said. "How are you?"

Greta didn't want Jesse to hear so she stretched the spiral phone cord to the bathroom and closed the door on it. She told Jeff what had happened with Daryl and the prostitute outside the Downtown Motel, that she called home and her dad came and got her.

"You mean you're here?" Jeff asked with a controlled excitement in his voice.

"Yes. I'm at my parents'," she said.

"That's why there was no operator. Oh, I'm so happy you're home," he said. "We can get on with our lives."

"I didn't know what else to do," said Greta. "It's just for now."

"You did the right thing," said Jeff. "Is there any chance I could see you tonight?"

"Sure, why don't you come over for dinner?" she suggested.

"Ok. I'll see you then," he agreed.

"See you later," she replied.

They said good-bye and hung up. Greta went upstairs to the kitchen where her mother was peeling potatoes.

She asked, "Is it ok if Jeff comes over for dinner tonight?"

"That's fine," answered Myra. "There's plenty."

Before going to the house for dinner that night, Jeff went to the garage where Sullo was tinkering on the snow blower.

"Good evening sir," he said to his elder.

"Well, hello there Jeff," Sullo replied.

"Greta invited me for dinner," said Jeff.

"I didn't know. I've been out here most of the day," said Sullo. "You can head on up to the house. I'm sure they're expecting you."

"I wanted to see you first sir. If you don't mind," said Jeff.

"That's fine. But I don't stand for formality. Just call me Sullo like everyone else does," he replied as he wiped his hands on a rag.

"Ok. Sullo. I've been talking with Greta some and she doesn't know yet but I'd like to ask her to marry me, with your permission of course," said Jeff with a quiver in his voice.

His face was beet red.

"Well, isn't that a nice surprise," answered Sullo. "I'd be honored to have you for my son-in-law. But there's something you should know before heading into such a proposal."

"I already know Sullo," Jeff replied. "I know that Greta is expecting."

"Oh, well then," Sullo smiled. "I can't answer for my daughter. But if she says yes, you have my blessing."

"Whew," said Jeff. "I was a little nervous about asking you."

Sullo wiped his husky hand on the front of his jeans and placed it on Jeff's shoulder.

"Just ask her when the moment feels right," he advised.

"Alright. I will," Jeff replied.

"I'm glad you're the baby's father," said Sullo.

Jeff didn't want him to know he wasn't the biological father. Feeling a little awkward about withholding the truth, he walked up to the house and knocked at the door.

"Come on in!" Myra hollered from the kitchen.

He opened the door and stepped into the entrance where he removed his boots and hung his jacket. Steam rose over Myra's face as she drained the water from a pot of boiled potatoes in the kitchen.

"Hello Mrs. Lehti," said Jeff.

"Go and have a seat in the living room," Myra said. "Greta will be up shortly to set the table."

"Alright," said Jeff.

He sat on the formal sofa and waited. Greta finally came up to the kitchen.

"Well it's about time you showed up. Jeff's waiting and you need to set the table," Myra barked.

"Ok," said Greta.

She set five places. Myra, Sullo, Jeff, Greta, and Jesse would be eating.

"I forgot to tell you Esther is coming. Make sure you set a place for her," Myra yelled from the kitchen.

"Ok ma!" she yelled back.

"You want something to drink Jeff?" Greta asked.

"No. I'm good thanks," replied Jeff.

Greta's waitressing skills came in handy as she quickly set the table and made sure there was a basket of bread and butter set out.

A tap-tap-tap came at the door and in walked Esther with some fresh cut flowers.

"Hello everybody!" she exclaimed in a cheerful voice.

"Oh my God Auntie!" Greta replied as she ran over to hug Esther.

"Hey kiddo. Good to see you," she replied. "Here, take these and put them in some water."

Greta found a heavy vase from the China cabinet, filled it with water and the little packet of plant food. She arranged the mixed bouquet and placed it in the center of the table. Then she joined Jeff in the living room while Esther helped Myra in the kitchen.

Sullo entered and went straight to the kitchen sink to wash his greasy hands with Palmolive.

"Where's Jesse?" he asked.

"Oh, probably watching tv downstairs," said Myra.

"Jesse! Get on up here! We're about to have dinner!" he called.

"Coming!" Jesse yelled back.

She ran up the stairs loudly and entered the kitchen.

"Hi auntie!" said Jesse.

"Hi hon. Can you put the mashed potatoes on the table please?" asked Esther.

"Sure," Jesse replied, taking the big bowl.

Jesse sat at her usual chair and scooped a large helping of potato onto her plate. Then she placed the bowl at the end of the table, close to where her father would sit.

"You may as well sit at the table now since the food is coming out," Greta told Jeff.

He got up from the sofa and sat in the seat across from Jesse while Greta helped in the kitchen. Soon after, Esther brought out a steaming bowl of peas and a plate of cabbage rolls. Myra entered the dining room with a dish of meatballs in one hand and macaroni salad in the other.

"Sit down now Sullo," she said.

"What about the skim milk?" said Sullo.

"I'll bring it dad," said Greta as she got the pitcher from the refrigerator.

"Let's give thanks before we eat," said Sullo.

As he bowed his head they all held hands in a circle. All sizes of hands, hardworking hands, soft hands and nervous hands embraced.

Heavenly Father, We thank you for bringing us together today. Thank you for the food we are about to eat and the hands that prepared it. Help us to do our best in the world for our family, friends, and neighbors. Teach us to respect all of your creation and forgive us when we go astray so we can return to the comfort and love of the bosom of our Savior Jesus Christ. Amen

In unison they said, "Amen."

Then Sullo said, "Let's eat."

"Dig in," said Myra.

"Looks great Mrs. Lehti," said Jeff.

"Jeff. Call me Myra," she replied. "You know us well enough by now. Don't you?"

"Ok Myra. It looks great and smells delicious," Jeff reiterated.

"Well, let us know how it tastes. Not how it looks," chortled Sullo.

The food was indeed delicious and plentiful. Greta cleared the dirty dishes and stacked them in the kitchen as the meal dwindled to an end.

"Ma, you want me to put the coffee on?" Greta asked.

"Yes please," Myra replied from the dining room.

Once the coffee began to brew, Greta took the dessert cake out of the refrigerator. It was a marble bundt cake with chocolate drizzle. "Who wants dessert with their coffee?" asked Greta as she brought out two slices on nice dessert plates.

"Me!" Jesse extended her hand.

"How 'bout you auntie?" asked Greta.

"I shouldn't. But I will," Esther replied with an outstretched hand.

"I'll have a piece with my coffee," said Sullo.

"None for me," said Myra who had only picked at her plate.

"I'll have a piece with coffee too please," said Jeff.

Greta put the cake on the dinner table and made sure everyone had a coffee cup and dessert plate. They sat and waited for the coffee.

"Greta?" asked Jeff.

"What?" she asked in return.

"How would you like to go for a walk after dinner?" asked Jeff.

"That would be nice," replied Greta.

She wanted to have a cigarette.

"So are you back to stay or are you just here for a visit?" asked Esther.

Greta felt nervous and embarrassed and didn't know what her aunt and mother had been talking about in the kitchen.

"I'll be staying here just until I can find a place of my own," replied Greta.

"Oh. Ok," said Esther. "So you're not going back to Circada?"

"She quit college," Jesse blurted out.

"Jesse, mind your own business," snapped Myra.

"It's ok ma," said Greta. "It wasn't as hands-on as I expected it to be and I couldn't get into it. So Jesse is right. I quit."

"Oh," said Esther. "Well that happens. Maybe you'll find something else you like better."

"Well for now I'm just going to look for a job," said Greta.

"I see," said Esther. "You could do some sewing for me. I've got clients waiting for pieces I'm working on. It would lighten my load."

"There are many options," said Myra. "We don't need to make any decisions right now. Do we?"

"I'll go check the coffee," said Greta as she got up quickly to avoid answering more questions.

It had finished brewing so she went around the table pouring for everyone except Jesse who was drinking milk with her cake.

"Thank you Greta," said Sullo.

Once she sat back down, she lowered her head and tried to avoid eye contact with her aunt for fear of being put on the spot again. Jeff casually stroked her outer thigh to comfort and reassure her of his presence. She looked over at Jeff and he smiled.

"Greta," he whispered.

There was a pause as she glanced towards him.

He continued, "You know how much I care about you and I've asked your dad if it's ok. It's entirely up to you but I hope you will."

Her face was questioning without words.

He paused again.

Finally he asked, "Will you marry me?"

As Greta's eyes sparkled. She wasn't quite sure she'd heard what she heard.

"Did you just ask what I think you asked?" asked Greta.

She realized that everyone was silent.

"Yes. Will you marry me?" he asked again.

He pulled out a plain gold band with a row of small diamonds from his pants pocket.

"It's not much. But my grandmother gave it to me before she died. And I want you to have it," he said.

Greta looked at the ring Jeff held in front of her and looked into his eyes as her own eyes began to well with tears of joy.

She said, "Yes. Jeff. Yes. I will marry you."

Sullo said, "That's nice."

He clapped his hands and everyone cheered.

Myra exclaimed, "Now I will have some cake!"

They laughed and cheered and Myra got out the camera and took a few pictures.

"Wanna go for that walk now Greta?" asked Jeff.

"Yes, I do," she replied.

"Practicing already eh," Jeff chuckled.

Myra, Sullo, and Esther were chatting in the living room now. They would have all the details of Jeff and Greta's wedding planned in short order. The only problem would be arriving at a consensus.

Jesse watched Greta and Jeff as they put on their boots and coats.

"So you're gonna be my brother now?" asked Jesse.

"That's right. Brother-in-law though," he replied.

"Cool!" exclaimed Jesse. "Where you gonna live?"

"We'll work out all the details later. But that's certainly something to talk about," he said.

"Come on hon," said Greta.

Greta tugged on the sleeve of his jacket.

The evening was still and their body heat kept them warm as they walked.

"I couldn't believe you asked me that in front of my parents," Greta said.

"I already asked your dad before dinner, but didn't know when it would happen," said Jeff. "He told me to ask you when the moment felt right."

They walked the silent rural roads that were lit by the occasional streetlight as a gentle fluffy snow began to fall. It was as if they were inside a magical snow globe, protected from everything and everyone else in the world.

And Greta said, "I think the moment is right, right now."

"Right for what?" asked Jeff.

"To tell you, I love you," said Greta.

They looked into each other's eyes as they stopped under a streetlight where they could see the fluffy flakes dancing around them.

Jeff said, "I love you too."

The kiss was awkward. It was like kissing a brother. He was too performative and unnatural; rigid instead of soft. He was moving his tongue too much instead of gently mouthing her lips.

He had won. They had all won. She was doing what they all wanted her to do, not what she wanted to do. Now she would have to keep the baby.

Scissors in Her Hand
by Sisko Linduska